The Mark on the Door

THE MARK ON THE DOOR

In their motorboat the *Sleuth*, Frank and Joe Hardy search Barmet Bay for a dangerous stranger who has stolen a valuable boat. Suddenly, in the eerie fog, they spot the craft drifting aimlessly out to sea. What happens next starts the young detectives and their pal Chet Morton on an intriguing adventure that takes them to Mexico and into the comparatively unexplored desert and mountain regions of Baja California.

The search for the meaning behind a mysterious symbol that terrorizes the people of an entire village, a daring escape from a submarine, perilous encounters with a band of renegade Indians, an unusual smuggling operation—all combine to make this one of the Hardys' most exciting cases.

As Frank and Joe turned round, another shot rang out!

THE HARDY BOYS MYSTERY STORIES

THE MARK
ON THE DOOR

By FRANKLIN W. DIXON

COLLINS · *London & Glasgow*

ISBN 0 00 160527 5

PRINTED AND MADE IN GREAT BRITAIN

CONTENTS

CHAPTER		PAGE
1	THE ATTACK	9
2	THE MISSING WITNESS	16
3	THE STRANGE SYMBOL	27
4	THE HOSTAGE	36
5	DANGER PATH	44
6	MYSTERIOUS VIGIL	52
7	NIGHT RENDEZVOUS	57
8	BULLFIGHT	62
9	THE TRAIL TO BAJA	69
10	A VILLAGER SPEAKS!	77
11	MOUNTAIN PURSUIT	83
12	THE SEARCH	92
13	A CHARGING DONKEY	97
14	A THREATENING MESSAGE	104
15	TUNNEL ESCAPE	113
16	FACE TO FACE	120
17	A HOT MÊLÉE	127
18	OUTWITTING A CREW	133
19	THE TRAPPER TRAPPED	143
20	HELICOPTER CAPTURE	151

·1·

The Attack

"Look! A periscope!" Joe Hardy shouted.

"Are you sure?" asked his brother Frank, who was at the wheel of their motorboat.

"You bet. Look over there!"

The Hardys were skimming across Barmet Bay in the *Sleuth*, checking it out before going on a fishing-trip to Maine with their father.

Frank spotted the thin, tapered metal mast to starboard, generating a tiny wake as it moved through the water.

"I see it now, Joe!"

"Let's take a closer look!" his brother cried.

Frank turned the wheel and advanced the throttle as they sped towards the periscope, but suddenly it sank beneath the waves!

Frank looked disappointed, and cruised around in a tight circle. "It must belong to the U.S. Navy."

"Maybe not," Joe replied.

The blond boy was seventeen, one year younger than dark-haired Frank. Both had learned from their detective father to be constantly on the alert.

A better instructor in police matters was nowhere to be found. Fenton Hardy, a former member of the

New York City Police Department, was renowned as a super-sleuth.

Frank and Joe had become so preoccupied with the periscope that they had failed to take notice of a speedboat approaching them from the rear. The craft made a close pass, then suddenly turned away so sharply that its stern skidded and struck the bow of the *Sleuth*. The boys hung on as sheets of water showered over them.

"What does that cowboy think he's doing?" Joe sputtered.

Frank rammed the throttle ahead and raced off in pursuit of the other boat. The *Sleuth* gained at first, enough for the Hardys to glimpse the name *Ira Q* painted on the stern. But the pilot of the fleeing craft applied more power and pulled away.

"That boat is too fast for us!" Joe shouted.

"I know," his brother agreed. "But I managed to get a good look at the guy behind the wheel. He looks Spanish. But the boat's name isn't."

"*Ira Q*? Never heard of it," Frank said. "Maybe it's just passing through."

"Perhaps. Anyway, I'm sure that speed demon is heading back to shore," Joe replied. "Let's go in and make some inquiries."

"We'd better telephone the Coast Guard Station and tell about that periscope too," Frank added.

The boys arrived at their private boathouse and tied up the *Sleuth*. An examination showed that she had a dent in her side. Then Frank went to a telephone booth and dialled the Barmet Coast Guard Station.

A man's voice crackled from the receiver. "Coast Guard. Lieutenant Parker speaking."

Frank told him what he and Joe had seen.

"Thank you for the information," the lieutenant replied. "Since no sub is expected here, I'll have one of our cutters start an immediate search!"

The respect and co-operation extended to the Hardys was typical of all who knew them. Frank and Joe often worked with their father on his cases, and their ability in solving baffling mysteries had won the youths an enviable reputation of their own.

After Frank had hung up, the boys made a reconnaissance of the piers and docks stretching along the shore of Barmet Bay.

Presently Joe grabbed his brother's arm. "I see the speedboat!" he said excitedly.

"Where?"

"At Sandy MacPherson's place!"

The boys ran to the dock of MacPherson's Boat Rental Service, where Sandy, an elderly Scot, seemed to be talking to himself.

"The brigand!" he stormed. "He bashed in the stern of me new boat! I've had the *Ira Q* but three days, and already it's damaged! He'll pay for this!"

"Who?" asked Frank.

"That Mexican fellow!"

"We're after him too," Frank said. "He damaged your boat when he ran into ours."

"What!" MacPherson exclaimed. "He'll no' get away with this!"

"Calm down, Mr MacPherson," Joe pleaded. "You say the fellow was Mexican?"

"Yes," the proprietor answered. "Pancho Cardillo was the name he gave me. He seemed to know quite a bit about boats. So I paid no mind when he asked me to rent him the *Ira Q.*"

"Did he give you an address?" Frank asked.

"Yes," MacPherson said. "He's at the Hotel Bayport. That's where he is."

"Thanks," Frank said. "Joe and I'll go there right away. This Cardillo fellow might suddenly get the idea to leave town."

After learning that Cardillo had driven off in a car, the boys hastened to their own convertible, which they had left near the boathouse. Frank headed for downtown Bayport. He parked in front of the hotel, then the young detectives darted into the foyer and approached the desk clerk.

"May we have Pancho Cardillo's room number, please?" Frank asked.

"You mean Señor Cardillo," the clerk replied. "He checked out just a few minutes ago. Paid his bill in pesos. Highly irregular. I had no alternative but to accept. Figuring out the exchange is always a nuisance."

Frank interrupted the clerk. "What address did he list in your register?"

The man glanced at his card file. "Tampico, Mexico," he answered. "And that's all I can tell you. The gentleman paid his bill and hurried to a car that was waiting for him outside."

"Can you give us a description of the car?" Frank prodded.

The clerk became irritated. "What do you fellows think I am—the FBI?"

"Well, thanks anyway," Frank said, and the boys hurried back to their own car.

Night had come on quickly, but Frank and Joe decided to make one more inquiry about Cardillo's car. If they had a description, Police Chief Collig could issue a bulletin to pick him up.

"I'd like to get my hands on that wise guy, if only for Sandy MacPherson's sake," Joe said. "He works hard to keep his boats in good condition."

Frank brought the car to a stop in front of a telephone booth. "I'm going to phone Sandy now. Just by chance, he might be able to give us a description of the car."

Frank dialled the boatman's number, but there was no answer. "That's funny," the boy remarked. "MacPherson doesn't answer—and he lives in the rear of his office."

"Maybe he's out on the dock and can't hear the phone ringing."

"Perhaps," Frank said. "Let's drive back there."

In a few minutes the boys arrived at MacPherson's dock. They noticed a dim, irregular pattern of light streaming through his office window, as if from a lamp that had been overturned. The boys hastened to the small building and peered inside.

MacPherson was lying face down on the floor.

"I think he's unconscious!" Frank exclaimed.

The Hardys rushed inside to help him. As they turned him face up, the boatman groaned. "That brigand! He was here again!"

"What happened?" Frank asked quickly.

"Cardillo came back! He wanted me speedboat. I

told him no. That devil said he would take the *Ira Q.* anyway."

"Easy now," Frank told the distraught man. "Then what happened?"

"I told him he'd have to step over me to get to it. He must've had friends with him, because I was suddenly hit from behind!"

Sandy MacPherson rose shakily and rubbed his head.

"Call the harbour police, Mr MacPherson!" Frank said quickly. "Joe and I'll take the *Sleuth* and search for your boat. There's a chance it still may be out on the bay."

"Watch out for fog!" MacPherson said. "It's forecast."

"We will," Frank assured him.

The boys drove to their boathouse, untied the *Sleuth*, and sped out onto Barmet Bay. Joe manned a portable searchlight, and swept the beam back and forth across the water.

"MacPherson was right about the weather forecast," Frank observed. "Fog is beginning to move in." Joe used the portable light intermittently so as not to be dazzled by its glare.

Nearly an hour passed. By now the Hardys were far out in the bay. They were about to turn back when Joe directed the beam of his searchlight slightly off the port bow.

"I've spotted something!" he exclaimed. "It looks like a boat!"

Frank swung the *Sleuth* towards the object. It presented a ghostlike image through the haze.

"It's the *Ira Q!*" Joe yelled triumphantly.

"Nobody's aboard!" Frank responded.

The boys guided the *Sleuth* alongside the craft. Joe was about to board it when three men suddenly sprang from behind the gunwale. One struck Joe on the head with a blow that sent him crashing back into the *Sleuth*. A split second later two of the men clobbered Frank. He slumped unconscious.

·2·

The Missing Witness

"WHAT—what happened?" Joe moaned as he regained consciousness.

Frank, still groggy, had already managed to get himself to his feet. "We were jumped by three men hiding aboard the *Ira Q.*"

"Cardillo must've been one of them," Joe surmised.

The boys reached into the salty water and bathed their bruises. Then they scanned the dark sea.

The mist had thickened and there was no sign of the *Ira Q.* Before they could start their stalled motor, the Hardys heard the piercing sound of a foghorn. It was followed by shouts.

"Ahoy! Ahoy! Is anybody out there?"

"Must be the harbour police!" Joe said.

The boys yelled in reply. Soon the running lights of the police boat loomed out of the fog. A small radar antenna revolved on top of a mast on the cabin roof.

"You must be the Hardys!" an officer cried. "Mac-Pherson said you were out here! We found his boat!"

The boys glanced over the stern of the police craft. In tow was the *Ira Q.*

"Did you find anyone aboard?" Frank asked.

"No. The boat was abandoned. We almost ran it down!"

Frank and Joe were mystified. Where could the three men have gone?

After telling the harbour police officers what had happened, the Hardys followed them back to Mac-Pherson's dock. Sandy, along with Police Chief Collig, greeted them.

"What's all this about?" Chief Collig asked, and was promptly brought up to date on the Cardillo case.

"There's not much to go on," the chief commented. "But I'll alert my men. Chances are those scoundrels will show up again."

The boys thanked the harbour police, berthed the *Sleuth* for the night, and drove home.

They were met at the door by their mother, a slim, attractive woman. "We've been worried about you— out in this fog," she said. "Oh, look at those awful bruises! What happened?"

"Nothing serious, Mother," Frank told her. "Joe and I just tangled with some crooks and came off second best."

"Crooks? Criminals, you mean!" The voice was that of Aunt Gertrude Hardy, a tall, angular woman who breezed into the room. "Good gracious! I hope you're not involved in another mystery!"

"Hello, Aunt Gertrude," Frank said with a grin. "Don't worry about us. We can take care of ourselves."

"Indeed!" Aunt Gertrude sniffed. "What about those bruises on your heads?"

"We just forgot to duck," Joe quipped.

"Oh! Teenagers!" Aunt Gertrude scolded. "Your

mother and I have been keeping a fine dinner warm. Come on. Sit down."

Gertrude Hardy, unmarried sister of Mr Hardy, had come to live at her brother's home. She was fond of her nephews, but thought that detective work was too dangerous for them.

The boys' mother smiled affectionately. "Yes. Come, eat. Aunt Gertrude made you an apple pie for dessert."

Frank and Joe had just finished their second helping of pie when Fenton Hardy arrived home.

"Hi, Dad!" Frank said cheerfully.

"Hello, boys. You look well fed."

"How was your visit to New York?" Joe asked as they went into the living-room.

"Fine," replied the tall, middle-aged detective. "I'd have been home earlier, but I had to take the train. The airport was fogged in."

Mr Hardy, youthful-looking for his years, greeted his wife, then sat in a large wing chair.

"Wait till you hear what happened to us today," Joe said. He recounted the stories about the periscope and the Ira Q.

"Very mysterious," Mr Hardy remarked. "And you say you saw the periscope in the bay? Maybe it had something to do with Cardillo."

Joe frowned in disbelief. "Do you think that's possible?"

"We'd have an awful time proving it," Frank said, "unless the Coast Guard comes up with something."

"What about the Sleuth?" their father asked. "Was it badly damaged?"

"A dent, that's all," Joe replied. "But not serious enough to keep us from our fishing-trip."

The detective leaned forward, slapped both his knees, and looked disappointed. "I'm afraid I won't be able to go." He sighed. "I must start working on the New York case right away."

"Oh no!" Joe exclaimed.

"Can you tell us about your case?" Frank asked.

Mr Hardy's brow creased. "It seems that a group of scoundrels has been peddling worthless stock in New York and New England. It has been sold in the name of a Mexican firm called Costa Químico Compañia. That's Spanish for Coast Chemical Company."

"I read something about that fraud," Frank interrupted. "Didn't several Bayport people buy some of the stock?"

"Yes. Like others, they were extremely gullible people who can be talked into a fast deal."

Mr Hardy told the boys that the authorities were not certain as yet how the fraud was being worked. However, the Securities Exchange Commission had filed indictments against three men in New York.

"But to get a conviction," the detective explained, "the authorities are depending on the testimony of Elmer Tremmer, a Bayport book-keeper who kept records for the swindlers. Tremmer's not too bright, but he's honest. It's believed he was innocently involved in the fraud."

"What's the problem?" Joe questioned. "Won't he co-operate?"

"On the contrary," Mr Hardy said. "I'm told he was eager to testify. Four days ago he went to New

York and checked in at a hotel. He was scheduled to appear at a preliminary hearing the following day. However, Tremmer disappeared shortly after his arrival and hasn't been seen since. My job is to try and find him."

"Do you think he was kidnapped?" Frank asked.

"Perhaps," his father replied. "Or scared off."

After Mr Hardy finished outlining his new case, it was late and the boys went to bed. Early the next morning they received a telephone call from their buddy Chet Morton.

"Hi, Chet!" Joe said. "This is a great honour—your getting up so early to phone us."

"Stow the funny talk. I called to ask if you and Frank are going out in the *Sleuth* today?"

"We didn't plan to, but we can. Why?"

"I'll tell you later. It's a surprise!" Chet announced excitedly. "Meet me at your boathouse in an hour, and you'll witness the marvel of the century!"

As the Hardys drove off to the rendezvous, Joe said, "What do you think Chet is up to?"

"He probably has some new hobby," Frank replied. "Whatever it is, we can be sure of one thing. It'll be good for a laugh."

Chet, plump and jovial, lived on a farm outside Bayport. He was always experimenting with one hobby or another. Many were short-lived, but once in a while they were useful for the Hardys in solving a mystery.

The young detectives arrived at their boathouse just as Chet came rumbling along in his father's farm truck. On the rear of it was an odd-shaped contraption hidden under a tarpaulin. Chet pulled up and hopped out.

"Now for the unveiling!" he announced. "If you fellows were wearing hats, I'd tell you to hold on to them real tight. You're in for a whale of a treat!"

He flung aside the tarpaulin with one swoop. Resting on top of two metal pontoons was a bare wooden frame, triangular in shape. At the apex was a delta-wing of thin, light fabric.

"Well, what do you think of it?" Chet asked proudly.

Joe stared at the contraption. "It's neat. But what is it?"

"You're looking at the Marvellous Morton Water Kite!" Chet said.

"Sounds impressive," Frank commented. "What does it do?"

"That should be obvious! My masterpiece will float on the water—see the two pontoons? You guys are supposed to tow me round the bay. Then, when we get up enough speed, the delta-wing will carry me into the air like a seagull."

"Pretty dangerous!" Joe muttered.

"Nothing doing!" said Frank. "That gadget looks too tricky to be handled by an amateur."

"Aw, come on," Chet pleaded. "I've spent a lot of time building this."

Chet was so persistent that the Hardys finally consented to tow him. But they urged their friend not to try anything fancy until he acquired some experience in controlling the kite.

While the Hardys untied the *Sleuth*, Chet changed into his swimming trunks and extended a long line of nylon rope from the kite to the *Sleuth*'s stern. Then he strapped himself to a small seat aboard the winged contraption.

"All set?" Joe yelled to his friend.

"Haul away!" Chet responded.

Frank advanced the throttle and the *Sleuth* moved ahead.

"Faster! Faster!" Chet shouted.

Frank increased speed, then he glanced back to see how the experiment was progressing. The fabric wing became rigid and the kite bounced a couple of times, then lifted a few feet off the water.

"Leaping lizards! Look at that!" Joe exclaimed.

"More speed!" Chet ordered.

Frank increased the power. Suddenly the kite went into an abrupt climb high above the water.

"Chet! Be careful!" Joe shouted.

At that instant the towline went limp and fluttered down towards the water.

"Help!" Chet shouted as the towline snapped.

"He's in free flight!" Frank yelled. "And gliding towards the shore!"

As the kite passed over land, a warm, vertical air current carried it up even higher. The boys watched helplessly as Chet vanished over the crest of a hill.

Speeding back to the boathouse, they leaped into their car and drove off in pursuit. Five minutes later Joe pointed to a knot of people peering at a factory chimney. Cries for help were coming from the stack. Chet was hanging on courageously.

Sirens wailed as the Bayport Fire Department and Police Emergency Squad vehicles screamed to the

"He's in free flight!" Frank yelled as the towline
snapped.

scene. Reporters and photographers rushed to record the rescue as Chet and his kite were untangled and brought to safety on a towering aerial ladder.

Chief Collig arrived to make sure the situation was under control. When he spotted the Hardys, he hurried over to talk to them.

"I tried to contact you boys a couple of hours ago," the chief said. "One of my men came across an unlocked car in a parking area near MacPherson's dock. No one knew who owned it, so we decided to run a routine check. The car was sold by a dealer in New York to a man named Pancho Cardillo! The address on the registration is fictitious."

"I'll bet Cardillo is not his real name either," Joe commented.

"If you boys would like to take a look at the car," Collig said, "you'll find it at the police garage."

"We'll do that," Frank answered.

The Hardys drove a subdued and badly frightened Chet back to his truck, then hastened to the police garage. There they examined the car minutely. Frank noticed a small object jammed underneath the accelerator. Pulling it out, he saw that it was a broken finger ring with a strange insignia on it.

"Look, Joe. Indian craftsmanship, I'll bet."

"Aztec, I'd say," Frank said.

The insignia was a cluster of faggots from which a flame issued, with a large letter P in the centre of the design.

"Maybe it's a family crest," Joe suggested.

Frank dropped the ring in his pocket. Then he and his brother drove home. As they entered the house, intending to show the ring to their father, he summoned them to his study. Mr Hardy was holding a white sheet of letter-size paper.

"This just came a few minutes ago," he said. "Frankly, I'm baffled. I don't know what to make of it."

He handed the letter to his sons. Their eyes widened when they saw the typewritten message:

BEWARE OF THE MARK ON THE DOOR!

·3·

The Strange Symbol

"WHAT mark on the door?" Frank asked. Joe hastened out to examine their front and back doors, and the garage as well.

"No signs there," Joe said when he returned.

"The envelope was postmarked Bayport," Mr Hardy said, "which brings the mystery right to our doorstep."

"It could be a prank," Frank said.

"You might be right," their father replied. "But I suggest we all be very careful."

As the boys took comfortable chairs in their father's study, Mr Hardy filed the mysterious warning and turned his attention to a thick dossier on his desk.

"I've been going over the information given me concerning the stock-fraud case," he said. "Very interesting. I'm sure you boys would like me to fill you in."

"We sure would!" Frank answered quickly as he and Joe pulled their chairs closer.

"I've already told you," the detective went on, "that the worthless stock was sold in the name of the Costa Químico Compañia."

The boys nodded.

"According to this information, the plan to start the

chemical firm was the idea of Señor José Marcheta, a retired chemical engineer and a highly respected resident of Vivira, Mexico."

"What made a man with his reputation go wrong?" Joe queried.

"That's just it!" the detective answered. "The facts indicate that Marcheta is not really part of the fraud."

He explained that the engineer was sincere in his efforts to create a firm for the refining of chemicals. His principal aim was not only to develop one of Mexico's great natural resources, but to bring work to the people of the area. It appeared, however, that Marcheta had become the target of extremely clever swindlers, who used his efforts as a front for a stock fraud.

"What does Señor Marcheta have to say about all this?" Frank asked.

"He was questioned by the United States consul in Guadalajara, Mexico," Mr Hardy explained. "He denied knowing anything about the scheme, or any of those involved."

"But he must know something about the men behind the plot," Joe insisted.

"I'm sure he does," Mr Hardy agreed. "Nevertheless, Marcheta isn't saying anything. And it's obvious why. The consul's report states that he appeared badly frightened. Whoever's behind the fraud must have come up with a strong enough threat to keep him from talking."

Frank and Joe mulled over the situation until bedtime. The next morning, Sunday, was chilly and rainy. The boys planned to do nothing more that day than to attend church, catch up on their reading, and ponder the mysterious events of Friday and Saturday.

After a leisurely lunch, the Hardys began to skim through the voluminous Sunday newspaper. Joe burst out laughing when he saw that Chet's water-kite escapade, complete with pictures, had made page two.

Frank was scanning another section when he suddenly sat bolt upright. "Wow!" he exclaimed, and quickly tore out a small news item. "Take a look at this!"

Joe's eyes widened in amazement at what he saw. The news story, datelined Mazatlan, Mexico, read:

A local fisherman has reported sighting an unknown submarine off the Sinaloa coast, approximately 140 miles northwest of Mazatlan. The sighting, according to police here, took place on Friday, but the report was not released at that time, pending an investigation by the Mexican Coast Guard.

Questioned by the authorities, the fisherman described an insignia painted on the conning-tower of the craft. In his words, it "appeared to be flames issuing from a bundle of sticks, with the letter P in the centre."

A spokesman for the Coast Guard said that a search revealed no evidence of a submarine in the area.

"It sounds impossible!" Joe said as Frank dashed to get the broken ring he had found in Cardillo's car. The boys showed it to their father, along with the clipping.

The detective was amazed as he examined the ring.

"Why, the design *is* similar to the one the fisherman described!"

"Exactly!" Joe exclaimed. "There must be some connection between Cardillo and the sub. Maybe he escaped in the one we saw in the bay."

"Now hold on a moment," Frank said. "If Cardillo did escape from Barmet Bay by submarine, it couldn't possibly be the same craft the fisherman spotted. It would take weeks for it to sail there!"

"You're right," Joe agreed. "But there could be more than one. What if Cardillo is a member of a gang that uses submarines?"

"Intriguing theory," Mr Hardy mused.

As they continued to discuss the mystery, the telephone rang. Frank scooped up the receiver. "Oh, hello, Chief Collig . . . What's that you say?" Frank listened for a few seconds, his expression taut with excitement. "Okay, Chief. I'll tell him. Goodbye."

Frank whirled round. "Dad! Joe! Listen to this! The chief said that one of his men from the crime lab examined Cardillo's car for fingerprints. It was clean except for one clear specimen on the handle of the right rear door. The print belongs to Elmer Tremmer!"

"That's a tremendous clue!" Mr Hardy cried. "This means Cardillo might have had something to do with Tremmer's disappearance!"

"Which suggests," Frank added, "that Cardillo could be mixed up in the stock fraud!"

"But what about the submarine angle?" Joe said. "There are faster and easier ways of escaping."

Mr Hardy rested back in his chair to think. "I'm beginning to believe there's more to all this than a missing book-keeper and the peddling of worthless stock," he said finally. "Also, the various bits of information we've collected so far have one thing in common —their connection with Mexico!"

Joe sighed. "That's a long way off."

"True," Mr Hardy said. "But it might prove worthwhile for us to go to Mazatlan."

"Us?" Frank cried out. "You mean Joe and me?"

"Of course. This is an important case. How about it, Joe?"

"Roger, Dad!"

"Señor Marcheta's home in Vivira is not far from Mazatlan," Mr Hardy went on. "I'd like to take a crack at talking to him myself. Perhaps I could get Marcheta to give me some useful information."

"And Joe and I can check on the fisherman's story," Frank suggested. "If we can track down the sub, you can be certain the trail will lead us to Cardillo . . ."

"And Tremmer!" Joe interjected.

"Exactly what I had in mind," Mr Hardy said. "Your lead is strong enough to make it worth the try. But since I'm working with the investigators of the Securities Exchange Commission, I'll have to get their okay."

Next morning Mr Hardy made a telephone call to a man in New York. He then joined his sons at breakfast to tell them that he had been given the green light to go to Mexico. Frank and Joe let out a loud cheer.

"Fiddlesticks!" Aunt Gertrude snapped as she placed a heaped platter of hot wheatcakes on the table. "Rushing off to the ends of the earth again! I just don't know what to make of this family."

"They're certainly on the go," Mrs Hardy said, serving the griddlecakes.

Joe laughed. "Mexico isn't so far off."

"But enough to cause your mother and me a lot of worry," Aunt Gertrude retorted. "I should think there'd be plenty for detectives to do right here."

Mr Hardy planned to use his own sleek, single-engine plane for the trip. He instructed his sons, both flyers themselves, to contact Jack Wayne, their pilot, to make arrangements. "Let's try to get off today," he said.

Joe rushed to the telephone. Soon he had Wayne on the line.

"Mazatlan, Mexico, you say? Hold on while I get my air charts." There was a brief silence, then the pilot's voice came on again. "As I see it, we'll have to make two refuelling stops. The first at Memphis, Tennessee, and the second at Brownsville, Texas."

"How long do you estimate the entire trip will take?" Joe asked.

"Roughly about fourteen hours of flight time to Mazatlan," Jack replied. "If we leave within the next couple of hours, we can be in Brownsville by eleven or twelve o'clock tonight, Texas time. Then we'll hole up there till morning. It'll not only give us a chance to get some sleep, but also we won't have to tackle those Mexican mountain ranges in the dark."

"Good! We'll see you at Bayport field as soon as we pack."

"One more thing," the pilot added in conclusion. "Mexico requires that everybody have a tourist card to visit the country. Also, I'll have to file a special flight plan to Mazatlan. But we can take care of all that in Brownsville."

Frank rushed into the room just as Joe finished his telephone call. "Guess what?" he said. "Dad suggested we ask Chet to go along."

"Great idea!"

Chet readily accepted and received permission from his father.

The Hardys began packing. Finally they were ready to leave for the airport. Mrs Hardy kissed her husband and sons as they said goodbye. She was aware of the dangers involved in their work, but seldom allowed her concern to be known to them.

Aunt Gertrude shook her head dolefully. "No good will come of this! Mark my words!" she prophesied. "But please be careful," she added, pecking the embarrassed boys on their cheeks.

Chet was ready when the Hardys drove up, and soon the group arrived at Bayport field. They found Jack Wayne seated in the plane. Within minutes the craft took off. The weather was exceptionally clear, and the terrain below presented a vivid picture in the sparkling sunlight.

The refuelling was made without incident, and it was nearly midnight when the Hardy plane touched down on the runway at Brownsville. Jack and the others wasted no time checking in at a nearby hotel.

After breakfast the next morning they went directly to the Mexican Tourist Bureau to obtain their tourist cards. Jack Wayne filed the necessary flight plan to Mazatlan and soon the travellers were winging off on the final leg of their flight.

Frank and Joe were particularly awed by the country over which they were flying. Beneath them was a mixture of open plains and bleached deserts. Mountains jutted up on all sides, and some of these seemed to Chet to be higher than their own altitude.

As they neared their destination the group gazed down on a solid layer of stratus clouds.

"Looks like bad weather rolling in from the coast," Frank observed.

Jack agreed. "I've been watching it. I'd better contact Mazatlan and see what's up."

The pilot switched on the radio. It crackled for an instant, then was silent. He turned on the stand-by radio. Nothing! Jack tapped the radio compass and other navigational equipment vigorously. "Oh, no!" he muttered.

"Trouble?" Mr Hardy queried.

"All our radios have gone out!" the pilot replied anxiously. "We must have a short in the electrical system."

"And we don't know what the visibility is like below that cloud layer!" Frank declared. "If it's zero-zero, we'd have to make an instrument approach. That's something we can't do without our radios!"

"At least we're west of the Sierra Madre Mountains," Joe commented. "We don't have to worry about running into those."

"What about turning round and going back?" Mr Hardy suggested. "The weather is clear east of the mountains."

Jack turned and scanned the area behind him. "I'm afraid that's out! Take a look yourselves!"

The Hardys and Chet turned to see a frightening sight. Towering cumulo-nimbus clouds—thunderstorms—were already developing along the windward side of the mountains.

"We could never climb high enough to get over those storms!" the pilot said. "And to fly through them would be suicide!"

"Then we're trapped!" Joe exclaimed.

·4·

The Hostage

FRANK frantically tried to get the radios working, while Jack Wayne flew in a continuous circle to maintain their position over Mazatlan.

"No good!" Frank finally declared. "We'll have to do the best we can without the radios!"

Chet groaned and Mr Hardy looked grim. Jack suddenly straightened the plane out on a westerly course. "I'm going to try something," he said.

"What?" Joe questioned nervously.

"The cloud layer doesn't extend too far out to sea," Jack answered. "I'm going to let down over the water in the clear. From there, we can see whether there's enough of a ceiling for us to get into Mazatlan."

The boys stared ahead as the pilot began his descent. After they had passed beyond the edge of the cloud layer, he dived the plane as low as he dared, then turned east towards the coast.

"We're in luck!" Frank exclaimed. "There's a ceiling of at least two or three hundred feet!"

"Yes," Jack agreed. "But the visibility isn't too good. However, if we're careful, we should be able to make it. Let's hope it doesn't get any worse."

The plane was now flying just above the surface of

36

the water. Frank and the others peered ahead into the mist.

Suddenly Joe pointed off to his left. "I see something out there! Or is it just a band of dark clouds?"

The pilot leaned forward in his seat. "That's the coast of Mexico!" he cried jubilantly.

As they flew closer, various features of the terrain became more clearly defined. Frank unfolded a chart and compared the coastline they were approaching with the map profile.

"That wide inlet directly ahead, with a peninsula of land jutting out from the left, matches the shape of the coastline on the map where Mazatlan is located!" he exclaimed.

Gradually a sprawling city began to appear out of the mist.

"It is!" Mr Hardy shouted. "Congratulations, Jack! You've hit it right on the nose!"

"Lucky again," the pilot said jokingly. He rolled the plane into a left turn. "The airport should be a couple of miles north of the city."

In less than a minute they spotted a bright, white rotating beam from a beacon on top of a building. Immediately adjacent to it, the outlines of runways began to take shape.

"There's the field!" Jack declared.

"I was never happier to see anything in my whole life," Chet sighed with relief.

"Since our radios are out, I can't communicate with the control tower," Jack explained. "I'll circle the field and wait for a green light."

The pilot had just completed two circuits of the

airport when a disc of green light glared from the tower. The pilot responded by banking the wings of the aircraft to the left and right several times. He then checked the wind tee to determine which runway was being used for landings. Shortly thereafter the Hardy plane touched down at Mazatlan.

In the terminal building the group underwent a routine check by customs officials, then Mr Hardy called for a taxi.

"There wasn't time to make hotel reservations in advance," he announced. "But we shouldn't have too much trouble at this time of year."

Soon the group was in a cab heading for the city proper. Despite the grey skies, the vivid green of the lush tropical scenery raised their spirits. As they sped along the Avenue del Mar, they could see the choppy waters of the Pacific and the mouth of the Gulf of California. People strolled slowly along the streets, men wearing colourful sarapes and women with rebozos draped over their heads and shoulders.

Arriving at a hotel, Mr Hardy dashed inside. He reappeared after a long wait. "The hotels are busier than I thought," he told Jack Wayne and the boys. "We'll have to take a suite. The clerk phoned several other places for me, but they don't have anything else either."

When they were ushered into the rooms, Chet plunked himself into a comfortable chair. "Now this is what I call real luxury," he said. "When do we eat?"

"Just as soon as we freshen up," Frank answered.

"Good! I'm not used to going without food this long," Chet complained. "We missed lunch, and my watch tells me it's almost time for supper."

Joe glanced at his chum's corpulent waistline. "You're stocked with enough reserve to last for weeks!"

Frank turned to his father. "What's first on your agenda, Dad?"

"A talk with Señor Marcheta," Mr Hardy replied. "In the morning I'll rent a car and drive to Vivira to see him."

"Meanwhile," Frank said, "Joe, Chet and I will try to locate the fisherman who reported sighting the sub. Perhaps the police will tell us where we can find him."

"I have my work cut out for me too," announced Jack Wayne. "I'll head for the airport first thing to-morrow to see about getting the radios repaired."

When they left the hotel to find a restaurant, the weather had improved and a magnificent sunset was visible. Palm trees swayed in a gentle breeze and the chatter of myna birds and parrots could be heard.

As the group strolled along, Chet gazed at the first seafood restaurant they came to with such a hungry expression that the others permitted him to lead them into it. After a hearty meal they walked back to the hotel. Chet, burdened down by the two large lobsters he had devoured, trailed behind the others at a snail's pace.

As they entered the foyer, the clerk at the reception desk handed Mr Hardy a message. The detective ripped open the sealed envelope, read the letter inside with a startled expression, and quickly handed it to Frank and Joe. They were equally surprised. The hand-printed message read:

GET OUT OF MAZATLAN, ALL OF YOU! YOU'RE IN GREAT DANGER!

Mr Hardy turned to the clerk. "Who gave you this message?"

"A boy came in with it about twenty minutes ago, sir," the clerk answered. "He said some man paid him two pesos to deliver it."

The Hardys and their companions hurried to their suite.

"Who could possibly know we're here?" Frank muttered as he examined the message again.

"Perhaps someone at the airport saw the flight plan I filed to Mazatlan," Jack Wayne suggested. "I not only have to list the number of passengers aboard, but also your father's name and address as owner of the plane."

"Even so," Mr Hardy commented with a puzzled expression, "no one here knows who I am."

"Tremmer does," Joe stated. "And that means Cardillo would also."

"I thought you fellows said that those guys left Bayport by submarine," Chet interrupted. "They'd have to travel like a rocket to beat us to Mazatlan."

"You're right," Frank said with a sigh. "But hey! What if Cardillo didn't stay with the sub? He might have travelled just a short way, then gone ashore near an airport where he could catch an airliner to Miami. From there he could fly direct to Mexico City, then by private plane, or feeder line, to Mazatlan."

"But if Cardillo intended to fly," Joe queried, "why bother with the sub at all?"

"That's a question I can't answer right now," Frank admitted.

"Maybe he suddenly discovered that he had claustrophobia," Chet quipped, "and couldn't stand to be boxed in."

"In any event," Mr Hardy announced, "we have to assume that Cardillo and Tremmer know we're here. And that calls for an immediate change in my plan! I'm going to try and see Señor Marcheta tonight. I hope it isn't too late already!"

"We'll go with you," Frank declared. "There may be trouble."

Jack Wayne was instructed to tend to the plane's radio repairs, while the boys leaped into a rented car with Mr Hardy.

"Vivira is less than forty miles north of Mazatlan," Frank said, examining a road map. "Just off the main road."

A little over an hour passed before the Hardys and Chet arrived in Vivira. It was a quiet little village with many trees, and a fountain in the centre of a small plaza. Standing near the fountain was a young man.

"*Donde esta el hacienda de Señor Marcheta?*" Frank asked the Mexican in his best high school Spanish.

The man did not answer. He eyed the Hardys and Chet for a moment, then pointed towards a large hacienda surrounded by a high stone wall at the far end of the street.

"*Gracias!*" Frank said.

"*Adiós!*" Chet called from the rear window.

At the spot the man had indicated, Mr Hardy and the boys got out of the car and walked towards a decorative wrought-iron gate. Set in the wall beside the gate was a metal handle. Joe gave it a hard yank and a bell tinkled. Shortly a slim, tall man appeared, silhouetted in the doorway of the hacienda.

"*Quién es ello?*—Who is it?" he asked.

"Are you Señor Marcheta?" Mr Hardy asked.

"*Sí!*"

"We're visitors from the United States. My name is Fenton Hardy. I'd like to talk to you."

"*Norte Americanos?* You wish to talk to me? Why?"

"Please, Señor Marcheta," the elder detective pleaded. "I won't take much of your time. It's important!"

The señor slowly walked towards his visitors. As he approached in the dim light the boys saw that he was an elderly, grey-haired man with a moustache and goatee. He had a kindly face and a manner that immediately commanded respect.

Mr Hardy introduced his sons and Chet. Marcheta studied them for a moment. "I cannot deny you the hospitality of my home," he said finally. "Come in."

He led the visitors into his hacienda and motioned to them to be seated. "Now what is it you wish to speak to me about?" he queried.

"I'll get right to the point," Mr Hardy said. "I'm working on a case connected with a stock fraud involving the Costa Químico Compañia."

Marcheta turned pale. "I have already been questioned by members of your consulate in Guadalajara!" he cried. "I tell you, as I told them, I have no information to give!"

"Señor Marcheta, please be patient," Mr Hardy

replied. "We're only trying to help you. If you can tell me anything at all—"

"No! I cannot!" the elderly man retorted. "You must understand. It is not for myself that I am afraid. I fear for the life of my son Juan. They have taken him away! I . . ." His words trailed off. He buried his face in his hands and sank into a chair.

"So that's it," Mr Hardy muttered. "Those scoundrels are holding your son as a hostage!"

"That should be reason enough for you to give us your co-operation," Joe put in.

"No, no!" Marcheta exclaimed. "I did not know what I was saying! You must go now!"

"We realize the situation you're in," Frank said solemnly. "But if you think you're going to help your son by keeping this to yourself, you're—"

At that instant a large stone came crashing through the window and landed in the middle of the room.

"What's that?" Chet cried.

"Everybody get down!" Frank shouted.

Mr Hardy pulled Marcheta out of his chair to the floor. Then Frank, followed by Joe and Chet, ran out of the house.

"Spread out and search the area!" Frank ordered. "Yell if you see anything!"

The boys groped their way through the darkness. As Frank neared the rear of the hacienda, a man suddenly sprang from behind a bush several yards away and pulled what looked like a coiled bullwhip from his belt. Then a long rawhide tentacle lashed out towards Frank!

·5·

Danger Path

SWISH! The end of the whip stung Frank's ankles and wound tightly round them! The man gave a sharp tug, and the boy crashed to the ground.

Quick as a cat, the man retrieved the whip and lashed out at a branch of a nearby tree. The slender tentacle coiled around the branch to form a clove hitch. As Frank scrambled to his feet, the intruder used it to swing himself, trapeze-fashion, to the top of the wall. The next instant he was gone!

The other boys came running. "What happened? Are you all right?" Joe shouted.

"I ran into the man we're looking for," Frank explained, rubbing his ankles. "And he's mighty handy with a whip."

The three boys returned to the hacienda to find Marcheta in a state of panic. "All is lost!" he cried. "I shall never see my son again!"

When Mr Hardy heard Frank's story, he handed the boys a piece of paper. "This was wrapped round the rock," he said.

On it was a drawing of flames issuing from a cluster of branches with the letter P in the centre. The symbol again! Under the drawing was a message written in Spanish. Translated, it read:

44

We are aware you have visitors! This could mean Juan's doom!

"Señor Marcheta," Frank said quickly, "do you know what this symbol stands for?"

"I do not! Nor do I care! The safety of my son is all that concerns me!"

"If you really mean that," Mr Hardy said, "you'll let us help you."

"It is because you are here that my son is in greater danger than ever!" Marcheta insisted.

Mr Hardy stroked his chin thoughtfully, and turned to the señor. "There's one way we might be able to protect your son—fight fire with fire. Señor Marcheta, you must go into hiding!"

"You mean leave here? Never! Never! Not while Juan is in their hands!"

"But it's for your son's sake," Mr Hardy urged. "If you were to disappear, the kidnappers would begin wondering what you're up to. Until they knew, I'm certain they wouldn't harm your son. He's their only insurance that you won't go to the authorities."

The señor nervously shifted in his chair. After thinking the plan over, he said slowly, "Perhaps you are right. But I will not leave Mexico."

"How about Mexico City?" Joe suggested. "It's easier to hide out in a populated place."

"Good idea," Mr Hardy agreed.

"What about Señora Marcheta?" Frank inquired.

"I sent my wife away for her own protection. Only I know where she is. As for your plan, it is a fine one. How do you propose to do it?"

"We'll have to figure out how to get you away without being seen," Mr Hardy explained. "Then you can be flown to Mexico City in my plane."

"But we can't risk going to Mazatlan Airport," Frank warned. "We already suspect that the gang has a spy there."

"How about having Jack fly here?" Joe said. "There must be lots of level country nearby."

"There is a large cattle ranch approximately six miles north of Vivira," Marcheta replied. "It is very flat and would be ideal for your purpose."

"Then it's settled!" Mr Hardy declared. "But to ensure absolute secrecy, we'll have Jack fly to the rendezvous point after dark. It's too late now, so it will have to be tomorrow night."

The Hardys outlined their plan. The detective and the boys would remain with Marcheta that night to make sure no harm would come to him. In the morning one of the boys would drive to Mazatlan to give Jack Wayne his instructions, then return to the hacienda to take Mr Hardy and Señor Marcheta to the cattle ranch.

"But there's still the problem of getting Señor Marcheta out of the hacienda without being seen," Joe commented.

"I've been thinking about that," Frank said. "And I have an idea."

"How about letting us in on it?" Chet urged.

"I'm almost the same height and build as Señor Marcheta," Frank declared. "If you will lend me some of your clothes, señor, I'll improvise a disguise that might fool whoever's spying on us."

"Could such a plan work?" the señor asked.

"It's worth a try," Frank replied. "Joe and Chet should go with me to make it appear that I'm in need of protection. We'll leave first thing in the morning."

The Hardys and Chet took turns standing guard during the night. In the morning Frank donned a suit of clothes Marcheta gave him, then ground some white chalk into powder and sprinkled it into his hair.

"Very clever," Marcheta commented with a grin. "Your hair is now almost as white as mine."

Next, Frank pulled a bit of stuffing from a worn chair, whitened it with chalk, and fashioned a moustache and a goatee for himself. A straw hat completed the disguise.

"You've done a terrific job," Mr Hardy said.

"Thanks, Dad. Keep your fingers crossed. I hope it works."

"Just one question," Joe interposed. "Whoever's watching the hacienda must know that there are five of us here. Won't it look suspicious if we don't all leave together?"

"I'm hoping he'll think that two of us stayed behind to nab him if he shows himself," Frank explained. He pulled the brim of the straw hat low over his eyes. "I'm all set to go! Hope this disguise works!"

The three boys hurried out of the house and made a beeline for their car. As they sped away, Joe, who was behind the wheel, glanced into the rear-view mirror and saw a man leap out from behind a tree.

"At least one villager is interested in our departure," Joe said. "I wonder if he's our man."

"We can't take the time to find out," Frank answered, and removed his disguise. Within the hour they arrived at the airport and quickly located Jack Wayne.

"Hi, fellows!" the pilot exclaimed. "You'll be glad to hear the plane's radios are working again. There was a defective circuit breaker in the system."

"Good," Joe replied. "We're going to need you and the plane."

The Hardys described their plan for the evening to Jack. When they had finished, the pilot told them how to set up the rendezvous point.

"Find a long, level stretch of ground. Make sure there are no obstructions near the spot. Then aim the headlights of your car in the direction you want me to land. Once I'm lined up, the plane's landing lights will show me the way."

"Try to make your departure as inconspicuous as possible," Frank said.

"I'll file a flight plan back to Brownsville, Texas," Jack replied. "That should confuse anyone who's curious. I can always cancel it later."

The boys drove into the city for a leisurely lunch. Then they went to their hotel to wait until dark. It was well into evening when Frank, Joe and Chet joined Mr Hardy and Señor Marcheta at the hacienda.

"Your disguise worked like a charm," the detective told Frank. "Shortly after you left, a man with a coiled bullwhip in his belt rode off on a horse. He certainly was in a hurry, judging by the amount of dust he was kicking up."

"We'd better get out of here," Joe warned. "He might decide to come back."

The Hardys and their companions got into the car

and took the road leading north from Vivira. Soon Señor Marcheta pointed to flat areas of land flanking both sides of the narrow road.

Frank pulled the car to a stop and got out, followed by Joe and Chet. Together they searched for a suitable landing spot, and found one that was flat and as smooth as a table. Frank returned to the car and manœuvred it to point in the direction Jack Wayne was to land.

Several hours passed before the droning sound of a plane's engine was heard. Frank switched on the headlights, then flicked them on and off several times. Minutes later the plane's landing lights illuminated the area ahead, and the craft touched down in a gentle landing.

Jack Wayne taxied the plane in and Mr Hardy and Señor Marcheta climbed aboard. Soon they were airborne. Chet and the young detectives watched as the plane disappeared in the night sky.

The Hardys and Chet drove back to their hotel in Mazatlan and turned in for several hours of sleep. After breakfast they went to the police station and asked for the name of the fisherman who had sighted the submarine.

The officer in charge told them that the report had not been kept on file and he himself had never seen it. He suggested, however, that they inquire along the docks.

The boys hastened to the area and made some inquiries. They had little success, until a Mexican youth, about Joe's age, approached them.

"Señores," he said, "excuse me, please, but I understand that you are looking for the fisherman who saw a submarine."

"That's right," Joe answered.

"My name is Tico," the Mexican boy extended his hand in greeting. "The man you seek is Señor Ricardo. He is now fishing and will not be back for two or three days."

The Bayporters introduced themselves and Frank asked if Tico knew anything about the fisherman's report.

"Only that he says he saw a submarine. I believe him, for I am sure that I have seen it too."

"You've seen a sub?" Chet blurted. "When? Where?"

"My father, who is also a fisherman, and I took our boat up the coast as far as Ensenada del Pabelion about two weeks ago," Tico explained. "On the way back I was certain that I saw what looked like a submarine in a cove."

"Why didn't you report it?" Frank asked.

"I had too small a glimpse of it to be sure what I saw," the youth replied. "It was nearly sunset, and my father insisted the shadows were playing tricks with my eyes. I forgot about it until Señor Ricardo said he saw a submarine a few days ago."

"You speak very good English," Chet commented.

"Thank you," Tico said with a smile. "My father sends me to a fine school in Mexico City. He does not wish me to become a fisherman, but perhaps a lawyer. I study English."

Frank thought for a moment. "Do you think you could find that cove again?"

"Yes—yes, I think I could do this," Tico assured him. "The cove is best reached by boat. Unfortunately my father is away fishing and I'm on my own for about a month. We have a small craft with an outboard that will serve our purpose. The journey will take about four or five hours."

"Good. Wait here for us," Frank said.

The Hardys and Chet first went to the Mazatlan shopping district to buy clothes suitable for their intended expedition. By the time the boys returned to the dock, Tico was in his boat, ready to depart. They hopped in, and the Mexican boy set off.

Frank and Joe marvelled at the scenery along the coast. It was extremely craggy and geysers of white foam shot up from the sea splashing against the jagged rocks.

Soon the wind became more brisk. The surface of the water grew choppy, and Tico had to increase the power to keep from drifting towards shore.

"It's blowing up a storm!" Joe warned. "We'd better beach this boat!"

"Too rocky!" Frank disagreed. "The boat would be smashed to pieces."

As the small craft was being tossed violently about, the motor mount suddenly pulled free from its fittings.

The entire unit disappeared into the water!

"*Caramba!*" Tico cried.

Frank and Joe found two paddles stowed underneath the seats. They grabbed them and made a valiant effort to keep the boat away from the craggy shore. But their attempt was futile. Despite their frantic paddling, the boat continued to be swept towards the jagged rocks!

· 6 ·

Mysterious Vigil

JOE'S paddle suddenly was ripped from his hands by the raging sea. The small boat was carried to the crest of a wave, and went skimming down the lee side towards the jagged rocks.

"Hang on!" Frank shouted as water spilled over the gunwales.

Suddenly the craft capsized and the four boys were tossed into the sea.

"Swim for it!" Frank cried. "Head for—!" He swallowed a mouthful of brine and coughed violently as he struggled through the maelstrom.

For a while the boys bobbed like corks in the turbulent sea, progressing for a few strokes, then being tossed back again. With arms flailing, they finally made it. Frank and Joe were the first to be hurled on to solid ground. Chet came next, followed by the Mexican youth.

Tico lay panting for a few minutes. "I am happy to see that everyone is all right," he finally said.

"Sorry about your boat," Joe remarked.

"It could not be helped," Tico said philosophically "Do not worry."

The boys walked a short distance inland. There the

52

wind was less brisk, and a warm sun began to send shimmering waves of heat up from the bleached sand and rocks.

"It's very desolate here," Frank observed. "Where are we?"

Tico took a moment to orient himself. "We are not far from the cove I spoke about," he said. "It is less than an hour from here on foot."

"No sense in turning back as long as we are this far," Joe commented.

The boys agreed to continue on. With the Mexican youth in the lead, they trekked ahead, and arrived at their destination in the time Tico had predicted.

"There it is!" he exclaimed. "I know by that tall point of rock. It looks over the cove."

They slowly worked their way down a steep incline of rock to the shore. At once the young sleuths began searching the area for clues.

"If a sub was here," Chet said, "you'd never know it. There's not a trace of anything but fish!"

He held his nose and pointed to a half-eaten sea trout that had been washed ashore.

Frank, passing a large rock nearly buried in the sand, noticed deep scratches on its surface. "Take a look at this, fellows," he called out.

"Hm! Looks like some kind of heavy objects were dragged over the ground," Joe stated as he studied the marks.

"Notice that they continue," Frank replied, "in a straight line towards that big boulder at the base of the incline."

As the boys began walking towards the spot, a shot

suddenly rang out! Then another! Splinters of rock sprayed in all directions.

"Jumping jackals!" Chet yelled. "Hit the dirt!"

Frank and Joe whirled to look up at the high rim of rock surrounding the cove. Two men, one taller than the other, mounted on horses, were silhouetted against the sky. Each carried a rifle, aimed in the boys' direction.

Bam! Bam!

Two more bullets struck nearby as the boys scrambled along the craggy shore of the cove.

"Quick!" Frank ordered. "In here!"

Followed by his companions, he darted into a narrow crevice. It led up the side of a steep hill and eventually opened into a place which served as an excellent vantage point. From there, the boys could look up and see their attackers clearly.

"Why did those men shoot at us?" Joe hissed angrily. "Are they bandits?"

Chet crouched low behind a rock. "I'm not curious enough to go out and ask them," he declared.

"Everybody be quiet!" Frank commanded.

They watched as the two men, dressed in ragged clothes and sombreros, got off their horses and scurried down the rocky incline to the cove.

"They're coming after us!" Tico whispered nervously.

"There are many crevices along the shore," Frank muttered. "Let's hope they don't find the right one."

Minutes ticked by slowly as the men searched. Once they came uncomfortably close to the boys' hiding-place. The taller man, his voice barely audible in the distance, said something to the other in Spanish. Then, apparently giving up the search, they climbed back up the rocky incline to their horses.

"Did you hear what that fellow said?" Frank asked Tico.

"It was difficult, but I heard most of what he said," the Mexican boy answered. "He told the other man that we were scared off by the shooting. They think we have run far from here by now."

"I wish I *was* far from here," Chet mumbled.

Frank suddenly pointed towards the men. "Look!" he blurted. "They're not getting on their horses and leaving. They're just sitting on the ground!"

"What are they up to?" Joe queried.

"Waiting for us to come back," Chet said ruefully.

"Maybe they're not waiting for us at all," Frank said. "But whatever the reason, we'll have to stay here till they leave."

Huddled in their hiding-place, the boys spent several agonizing hours under the hot sun. By now their clothes were practically dry. But they were hungry, thirsty and exhausted by the intense heat. Even after sunset the armed men maintained their vigil.

"Are they going to sit there all night?" Chet grumbled. "I want something to eat!"

"When it is very dark," Tico said, "perhaps we can sneak away without being seen."

Frank now appeared less anxious to make an immediate getaway. "I'd like to stick around a little while longer and see what those two guys are up to," he announced. "We might learn something interesting."

Another hour had passed when a muffled, rumbling sound drifted in from the sea just beyond the cove.

"What's that?" Chet asked, craning his neck to look out.

"Sounds like engines," Joe said. "Get down, Chet!"

Suddenly a point of light began flashing from the position where the men were sitting.

"They're signalling someone!" Frank observed.

Carefully they turned to look out into the cove. A flashing light pierced the darkness in response.

Gradually the rumbling became louder. Chet's eyes popped and Joe gasped as the faint outline of a submarine slowly approached the cove!

·7·

Night Rendezvous

THE boys gazed fascinated as the submarine drew closer to the shore.

"It's hard to believe," Frank whispered excitedly, "but there it is!"

"Leaping lizards!" Chet gasped.

"So that's what those two bandits were waiting for," said Joe.

All at once there was a burst of activity on the deck. Flashlights, carried by members of the crew as they scurried about, looked like a swarm of agitated fireflies.

"*Pronto! Pronto!*" a crewman barked. Then came an incoherent mumbling of many voices.

Beams of light were directed at the big boulder which Frank and Joe were about to examine when the two armed men had fired at them.

"Come on! Push this thing aside!" shouted a crewman in English. "Hurry it up!"

Four husky fellows shoved the rock to one side. Behind it was a large cavity in the incline. Despite their distance from the hole, the boys could clearly see stacks of wooden boxes in the hiding-place.

"The cove is a rendezvous for picking up some sort of supplies," Joe said.

Frank remarked that it was too dark to see whether the strange symbol was painted on the conning-tower, but Joe had an answer for that.

"I'll sneak down to the cove for a closer look."

"I'll go with you," Chet offered.

"No, it's better if only one of us goes."

Joe slowly worked his way down through the crevice, then quietly stole along the craggy shore towards the submarine. Crawling on hands and knees, he made his way to a jumble of rocks near the water's edge. Joe crouched down and peered over the damp rocks.

"Keep movin'. Get that stuff aboard!" ordered a bearded, heavy-set man wearing a battered visor cap. It was obvious to Joe that he was not a Mexican. Neither were most of the other crewmen, who carried the wooden boxes to the sub.

Then one of the riflemen approached the bearded man. "*Qué tal van las cosas*—" the Mexican was saying.

"Talk English!" the other snapped. "You know I can't speak much Spanish."

"*Sentirlo*—sorry. I do as you wish, señor."

Loud enough for Joe to hear, the Mexican told of spotting the boys in the cove. "But we scare 'em off. We have no trouble."

"That's what you think!" Joe told himself.

"It doesn't matter," the bearded man went on. "We've got all the supplies we need and won't be comin' back here any more."

"What about me and my *amigo*?" the Mexican inquired.

"The boss needs more men back at headquarters. He said you and your friend were to go back with us.

We'd better get goin' cause the trip takes about twelve hours."

The crewmen hurried to load all the boxes aboard. The beam of one flashlight swept across the conning-tower and Joe squinted intently to get a glimpse.

There it was! *The same mysterious symbol!*

Joe tingled with excitement. The identical sub, or a sister ship at least, both here and in Barmet Bay!

Satisfied that he had seen and heard enough, he decided to rejoin his companions. As Joe moved, his hand brushed against a loose rock. It splashed into the water loud enough for the crewmen to hear the sound.

"What was that?" one man shouted.

Joe froze, waiting anxiously while beams of light crisscrossed the shore.

"See anything?" another asked.

"Naw. It must've been a fish."

"Okay!" the bearded one shouted. "Let's get goin'! Cast off the lines!"

The two riflemen unsaddled their horses and sent them galloping off on their own. Then they quickly boarded the submarine.

Joe gave a sigh of relief and crept off. By the time he returned to his companions, the sub was already on its way out of the cove. Breathlessly, Joe related his findings to the others.

"I wonder where it's headed," Chet said.

"That's anybody's guess," Joe replied.

"The bearded guy said it would take twelve hours to get where they're going?" Frank queried.

"Right," Joe replied. "But in that time the sub could be anywhere from one hundred to more than two hundred miles away, depending on whether the trip is made submerged or on the surface."

"What do you think are in those boxes?" Tico asked.

"Hard to tell," Joe said, shaking his head. "They appeared to be heavy. I'd say they contain metal tools, or maybe parts for machinery."

"This is one of the craziest situations I ever saw," Chet declared. "A sub sneaks into a cove at night to pick up a lot of wooden boxes hidden in the rocks. Why not use a regular boat?"

"Secrecy for one thing," Frank replied. "Obviously it's a renegade sub. And—"

"And you can be sure," Joe interjected, "that it's being used for something more than just hauling cargo around."

"And then there's the question of Cardillo," Frank said. "How does he fit into the picture, if at all?"

"Before you masterminds begin building up a case," Chet interrupted, "how about giving some thought to our food and water problem?"

Joe glanced at the luminous dial of his wristwatch. "It'll be light in a couple of hours. We'd better wait till then before we go trekking around the country-side."

"That is wise," Tico agreed. "We would gain little by trying to make our way through the darkness."

The four boys stretched out in the shelter of some scrubby bushes and fell fast asleep. At the first light of day they awakened and began climbing up the steep, rocky incline. They rested at the top for a moment and peered across the parched and barren plain.

"There isn't much to eat and drink out there," Chet muttered.

"There's lots of cactus around," Frank said. "That'll take care of our water problem."

"And we are sure to find plants which can be eaten," Tico added, "such as *acerolo*."

"*Acerolo?*" Chet blurted.

Joe explained, "It's a plant which bears small red and yellow apples. They're very good."

As the sun rose higher, the boys' hunger and thirst grew more intense. Tico led his friends to a cactus plant, removed a fisherman's knife from his belt, and sliced off the top. He dug out some of the pulp from which he squeezed a small quantity of water.

"You certainly picked a good one," Frank remarked with a grin.

As Tico began digging out more pulp for his friends, he saw Chet, a sharp stone in his hand, working on another cactus plant.

"*Caramba!*" the Mexican youth screamed. "Do not touch that plant! It is *muy malo*!"

Chet was startled. "It's what?"

"Very bad!" Tico shouted. "The liquid is poison!"

"Poison?" Chet muttered nervously. His face turned pale. "Why—why, I've already drunk some of it!"

·8·

Bullfight

Tico and the Hardys rushed to Chet. He staggered around, as if in great pain, and gripped his chest. "I don't feel too well," he said in a quavering voice.

"We must do something!" Joe yelled frantically.

"The nearest doctor will be miles away!" Frank said.

Suddenly Tico pointed to a figure in the distance. "I see something! I believe— yes, it is a man on a horse!"

"Oh, oh!" Joe muttered. "Maybe he's a friend of those two guys who shot at us."

"That's a chance we'll have to take!" Frank said.

The Hardys and Tico waved their arms wildly and called out to the distant rider. Finally he headed in their direction.

"*Buenos dias!*" the horseman shouted as he rode up and dismounted. He was short and wiry and had a handsome face.

"*Necesitamos un doctor!*—We need a doctor!" cried Tico.

"*Qué pasa?*—What is going on?" the stranger asked.

Tico quickly told the man what Chet had done and pointed to the cactus plant. The man walked over to it, studied the plant for a moment, then he scooped out some of the pulp and squeezed the liquid into his mouth.

"Hey! What are you doing?" Joe yelled.

The man grinned. He glanced at the Hardys, then at Chet, who by this time was rolling on the ground. "Americanos?" he inquired.

"Yes!" Frank replied, and added, "You speak English?"

"I do," was the calm reply.

Chet moaned and his eyes rolled. "Please help me!" he pleaded. "Just don't stand there and talk."

Tico turned excitedly to the horseman. "Why did you drink from the poison cactus, señor?"

"The water is good," the man said. "The plant looks like a poisonous kind. But it is not."

They all sighed, and Chet blurted, "Are you sure?"

"I am," the man answered.

Chet recovered quickly and got to his feet. "I—I guess I am all right, after all," he said. "Boy! That was a bad scare! Thank you, Señor—"

"Alvaro Cortines Garcia," the horseman announced with a courtly bow.

"How do you do, Señor Garcia?" Frank said. He introduced himself and the boys.

"We never expected to see anyone out here in the desert," Joe remarked. "You certainly surprised us."

"I am returning to my *ranchero* from the town of El Dorado," Garcia said. "My hacienda is about six miles from here, near the village of La Brecha."

Garcia told the boys that he bred horses and burros on his small ranch. He had gone to El Dorado to close a business deal involving the sale of some of his stock.

"I would like to offer you *muchachos* the hospitality of my home," the horseman added. "You all look very tired."

The boys did not have to be coaxed. They immediately accepted the offer.

By taking turns riding Señor Garcia's horse, the travellers had time to rest their exhausted bodies. Nearly two hours later they arrived at the adobe-walled hacienda. It was set in a green patch of semi-desert, surrounded by poplar trees nearly as high as the twirling windmill.

The dusty boys hastened to a trough of sparkling clear water at the base of the windmill. After gulping handfuls of water, they splashed their arms and faces.

As they finished refreshing themselves, a pretty woman and a good-looking boy of about sixteen came from the house. Señor Garcia introduced them as his wife and son Alfredo.

Tico and Alfredo began to chatter in Spanish. The visitors were ushered past the corral and inside the cool hacienda. Here Señora Garcia asked a maid to set the dining-room table and prepare food for the visitors.

Garcia sat with the hungry boys while they were eating. Presently he said, "We must give a little fiesta tonight to celebrate my success in El Dorado!"

"*Bueno!*" declared Alfredo. "We will invite some of our *amigos* from the village." His father turned to the boys. "And you, *muchachos*, must stay as my guests."

"I'm all for that!" Chet exclaimed, beaming. "*Muchas gracias!*"

After a long nap, the Americans spent the rest of the

afternoon watching preparations for the fiesta. They helped set up large wooden tables on the patio. Bananas, oranges, limes and avocados were heaped on some of the tables. Food that was cooking gave off tantalizing odours.

"This will be a gastronomic adventure!" Chet exclaimed as he viewed the preparations hungrily.

Joe grinned. "We might never get Chet to leave this place!"

Guests from the village began coming shortly after sunset. As the festivities got underway, torches were lighted to illuminate the area. One man arrived leading a bull and put it in the corral. Many of the younger villagers swarmed around the enclosure to see it.

"What's going on?" Chet asked Alfredo.

"Some of our *amigos* like to show their skills as matadors," he replied.

"Bullfighting?" Joe asked.

"They are not real matadors," Alfredo explained laughingly. "It is just a game. The bull does not have sharp horns, and he is not harmed in any way."

The boys hurried over to the corral and saw that one young man had already leaped into the enclosure. He waved a *muleta*, a small red cloth draped over a stick, in front of the bull.

"*Toro! Toro!*" shouted the would-be matador.

The animal rushed towards him, but the young man side-stepped gracefully.

"*Olé! Olé!*" the spectators cheered.

The boys watched the fun for several minutes. Then as Frank and Joe walked back to the tables they suddenly became aware of Chet's absence.

"*Toro! Toro!*" came their pal's voice from the corral.

"Oh, no!" Joe yelled. "Don't tell me Chet's playing matador!"

As the Hardys ran back they saw their hefty pal inside the enclosure waving a *muleta*.

"Get out of there!" Frank shouted. "Or we'll have to carry you out in pieces!"

At that instant the bull rushed towards Chet, who side-stepped. But he lost his footing and fell to the ground. The bull sped on past and turned to make another charge.

Chet scrambled to his feet, dropped the *muleta*, and began running. The bull raced after him and the spectators cheered.

"Head for the fence!" Frank yelled.

Chet did not hear. Instead, he kept running in circles with the bull in pursuit. Finally he made a dash for the fence and tried to force his way between the wooden slats, but he got stuck!

"Watch out for the bull!" Joe warned.

He flung himself over the fence, picked up the *muleta*, and attracted the animal's attention away from the panting Chet. Several spectators leaped into the enclosure to help.

With the bull diverted, Frank and Tico pulled Chet loose. The only damage was a couple of buttons missing from his shirt.

"Do you still want to be a matador?" Frank asked with a frown.

"I'll stick to football," Chet muttered.

"That waistline of yours almost got you into real trouble with the fence," Joe added.

"Yes, and now I'm hungry again," Chet said. "Let's have some chow."

It was after midnight when the fiesta ended. After the villagers had left, the boys and their hosts sat on the patio of the hacienda to chat.

"We enjoyed the fiesta very much, Señor Garcia," Frank said.

"*Gracias,*" the man replied. "And you are all welcome to stay here as long as you wish."

"We'd like to," Joe said apologetically, "but we must get back to Mazatlan as soon as possible."

"I'm sorry you can't remain longer," Garcia said. "But if you must leave, I will help you. There is an autobus which travels to the city along a road about fifteen kilometres east of here. I will furnish you with horses and take you there myself."

"Thank you," Frank said. "Could we leave in the morning?"

"Of course," Señor Garcia replied.

"Señor, are you familiar with the Sinaloa coast near the spot where you found us?" Joe queried.

"Yes, I travel along it many times on my way to El Dorado," Garcia answered.

"Have you ever seen a submarine in the area?" Joe continued.

"A *submarino*?" the man muttered with a quizzical expression on his face. "No, I have not."

Frank grinned. "I know it sounds like a strange question, but we have good reasons for asking."

"I do not think it strange," Garcia assured the boys. "I am certain the navies of many countries sail into our waters from time to time. Why do you ask?"

"We'd rather not say at present," Frank replied. "But we're sure the submarine we asked you about does not belong to any navy."

"This sub has a mysterious insignia painted on its conning-tower," Joe explained. He leaned down and outlined the symbol in the sand.

Señor Garcia studied it in the light of the flickering torches. Suddenly he leaped to his feet. "*Caramba!*" he cried, and an expression of fear spread across his face.

"What's wrong?" Joe asked, startled.

"You must leave here at once!" the man shouted.

"What do you mean?" Frank asked.

"I say you must go!" Garcia demanded. "You might have brought the curse of the symbol to my home!"

· 9 ·

The Trail to Baja

"CURSE of the symbol?" Frank blurted. "What do you mean?"

"I do not wish to talk about it!" Garcia snapped. "You must all leave!"

"But you can't just order us out into the desert in the middle of the night," Joe said angrily.

At that moment Garcia's wife intervened. She pleaded with her husband to let the boys stay until morning, and he reluctantly agreed.

The four companions were led to a *jacal*, a hut, which contained several empty bunks. Chet and Tico dozed off immediately, but Frank and Joe remained awake for some time discussing Garcia's strange behaviour.

"What could be bothering him?" Joe questioned. "He looked scared out of his wits when I outlined the symbol."

"Obviously it has some connection with a fright he's had," Frank surmised. "I wish we could get him to tell us about it."

"From his reaction, I'd say our chances are nil," Joe said.

In the morning the Hardys were relieved to find that

Señor Garcia had calmed down considerably. He even invited them and their friends to have breakfast with him.

"I must apologize for my behaviour last night," he said. "As I promised, I will guide you to the road where you can board the autobus to Mazatlan."

After eating, Garcia and the boys started out on their journey. It was early afternoon when they arrived at their destination, a narrow, unpaved road stretching north and south through a lonely expanse of desert country.

"Only one autobus a day travels this road to Mazatlan," Garcia explained. "It should pass this way within the next hour or two."

While they waited, Frank decided to take another chance at questioning their host.

"Señor, I don't want to upset you again," he said, "but is there nothing you can tell us about the symbol?"

Garcia glared. "No! There is nothing!"

Then, without mentioning Marcheta by name, Frank described how the engineer's son had been kidnapped. "He is about your own son's age. And we suspect that there's some connection between the symbol and the kidnapping. If you tell us what you know, it may solve this mystery."

Garcia did not reply. He stared blankly into space for a long moment, then said, "I am a coward for not speaking. Perhaps I should have gone directly to the authorities."

"What do you mean?" Joe queried.

"You must first promise that you will not reveal who

told you what I am about to say," the rancher declared.

The Hardys nodded.

"Several weeks ago," Garcia continued, "I went to visit my cousin who lives in the village of Montaraz in Baja. But when I arrived there I was told that he had mysteriously disappeared the day before. Painted on the door of his hacienda was the symbol you described to me."

"Did you speak to any of the villagers about your cousin's disappearance?" Frank asked.

"Yes, I tried to. But they were all badly frightened and refused to speak."

"What were they frightened about?" Joe asked.

"I learned that five other men in the village had also vanished in the same way," Garcia answered. "And the symbol was painted on the doors of *their* haciendas!"

"Why didn't you notify the police?" Frank questioned.

"I intended to do so, of course," the man answered. "But there are no police in Montaraz. I therefore planned to go to the city of Ensenada the following day to notify the authorities. I went to my cousin's to spend the night and the next morning found a message under the door."

"What did it say?" Tico asked.

"It warned me that if I talked to the authorities," Garcia said nervously, "the curse of the symbol would find me wherever I go!"

"Leaping lizards!" Chet exclaimed.

"I am not a cowardly man," the rancher continued,

"and it is not for myself that I am frightened. I fear for my family!"

"We understand," Frank said sympathetically.

Soon the bus arrived. The boys thanked Señor Garcia for his hospitality, then boarded the bus for the bumpy, dusty ride back to Mazatlan. When they reached their hotel, the desk clerk handed the Hardys a telephone message. It read:

Remaining with our friend for a while. Will contact you later. F.H.

"Dad's staying with Señor Marcheta in Mexico City for a while," Frank said as he handed his brother the message.

"I hope he's not running into trouble," Joe replied.

"I don't think so," Frank said. "He's probably hoping to worm more information out of Marcheta."

"When do we eat?" Chet interrupted.

Frank grinned. "Tell you what. The hotel has room service. Why don't we have supper in our suite?"

"Good idea," Joe agreed. He turned to Tico. "And you must join us as our guest."

"Thank you," the Mexican youth answered. "I would like to very much."

The boys had a hearty dinner, after which Frank unfolded an air chart of Mexico.

"Here's Montaraz, the village where Señor Garcia's cousin disappeared," Joe said eagerly. He inspected the map more closely. "Sure is rugged country. The desert area covers about six thousand square miles, I understand."

"And many of the mountains to the east are comparatively unexplored," Tico added. "One could easily disappear in that area and, perhaps, never be found."

Frank took out a pair of measuring dividers and calculated the distance to the village. "Hm! We might be on to something," he said, and thought for a moment. "Let's assume that the sub we saw in the cove maintained an average speed of twelve to fifteen knots. In twelve hours it would reach a point on the east coast of Baja not too many miles from Montaraz."

"Wow!" Chet exclaimed. "This could be an important lead!"

"At least it's worth checking out," Frank concluded. "Why don't we go there and see what we can find?"

"Too bad Dad's plane is in Mexico City," Joe remarked. "We could fly there in two hours."

"There aren't any airports near the village," his brother observed as he examined the chart. "Anyway, it would be less conspicuous if we went by boat."

"Maybe we can rent one," Joe suggested.

"I can be of help to you," Tico put in. "A friend of my father's has a boat-rental service. He can provide you with a small cabin boat. But you must let me come with you. I have some knowledge of the waters in the area."

"It's a deal!" said Frank.

Early the following morning the boys prepared for their trip. Before departing, the Hardys left a message for their father with the desk clerk. It read:

Gone Fishing. Wish us luck. We should be back in two or three days.

Tico proved to be an excellent seaman and navigator, and they made the journey in record time. As the craft neared its destination, the boys scanned the craggy coastline for a place to land.

Joe examined a map. "Montaraz is about six miles inland from our present position. We'd better find a place to tie up near here."

Just then Chet pointed towards the shore. "I see a little hut! And a small boat's tied up to a dock in front of it!"

"There's a man, too," Joe said.

The boys headed towards the spot. As they drew nearer, they saw that the dock was in a run-down condition. The hut was also decrepit and appeared undecided as to which way it was going to fall.

"*Buenas dias, amigo!*" Frank shouted to the elderly man who was resting against a *cirio* tree.

The old fellow raised the brim of his sombrero and peered at his visitors.

"Do you speak English?" Joe called out.

"He does not understand," Tico observed. "I will talk to him."

The Mexican youth chatted with the man for several minutes. He then returned to his friends. "The old man lives here by himself," Tico explained. "He says we may use his dock for eighty pesos a day."

"Did you ask him the way to Montaraz?" Frank inquired.

"Yes. There is a trail behind his hut which will take us to a road leading to the village. But I am afraid we will have to walk, since there is no transportation available."

"Oh, no!" Chet bellowed.

The boys started off on their journey, taking with them an emergency kit of camping equipment, food and water. It was almost sunset when they reached Montaraz. The village, consisting of about sixty adobe-walled houses, appeared quiet and peaceful.

Most of the structures surrounded a wide, circular piece of ground which served as the plaza. On the south side of the plaza was a sun-baked mud-brick building that served as a *cantina* and general store. There were no villagers in sight.

"Where is everybody?" Joe queried.

"I don't know," Frank muttered with a puzzled expression.

"Perhaps we will find someone in the *cantina*," Tico suggested.

The boys strolled over to the structure and found two of the villagers inside. They were middle-aged men and wore sombreros and colourful sarapes. Tico conversed with them in Spanish. Then he turned to the Hardys and Chet.

"The men say that the people of their village all remain in their haciendas from sunset to sunrise," the Mexican youth said. "It is because they fear Pavura!"

"Pavura?" Joe questioned. "What's that?"

"It means 'terror'," Tico said. "The men also say that we should leave because strangers are not welcome here. Anyway, there is no place for us to stay."

"That's hospitality for you," Chet grumbled.

Tico tried to question the villagers further, but he and the other boys were ordered out of the *cantina*.

"It's a cinch we're not going back to Mazatlan

without trying to get some information," Frank said angrily.

"Why don't we make camp for the night," Joe suggested. "Maybe we'll have better luck in the morning."

The boys pitched their tents on the outskirts of the village, then prepared supper from a variety of canned foods included in the camping kit. Soon after eating, they all fell asleep. The following morning the young sleuths got ready to return to the village.

"Chet," said Frank, "you stay here and break camp. Tico, Joe and I will go in town and see what we can find out."

Several villagers were walking about when the boys arrived in the plaza. It was impossible, however, to get any of the people to talk.

"Whatever, or whoever, this Pavura is," Joe remarked, "it sure has these villagers scared."

As they continued walking, Frank suddenly pointed to one of the houses. "Look!" he declared. "That must be the home of one of the villagers Señor Garcia told us disappeared. There's the symbol painted on its door!"

They walked forward to examine the door more closely when a stocky Mexican man seemed to appear from nowhere and blocked their path.

"Who are you?" Joe demanded.

The man did not reply. He drew a large, gleaming machete from his belt and raised it threateningly!

·10·

A Villager Speaks!

"*Váyase ustedes!*—Leave here!" the man with the knife shouted.

"*Por qué?*—Why?" Frank retorted.

The Mexican pointed to the symbol painted on the door. He then let go a volley of words so rapid that even Tico had difficulty understanding him.

"What's bothering him?"

"He says that the presence of strangers in the village will bring Pavura down upon them," Tico explained. "He wants us to leave at once."

The man wielded the machete menacingly.

"Let's not push the issue," Frank advised. "It would only make things more difficult for us if we got involved in any trouble."

The man glared at the boys as they walked off.

"I don't think we're going to get any information out of these people," Joe concluded, disappointed.

"But there must be at least one villager with enough courage to talk," Frank said.

"Garcia said there aren't any policemen here," Joe commented. "How do they keep law and order?"

"Usually the elders of a village appoint a man to be, what you call in your country, a sheriff," Tico explained.

"Then why don't we find out who he is and ask him some questions?" Joe suggested.

"Good idea!" his brother replied.

At the Hardys suggestion, Tico approached an old man they spotted walking across the plaza. After a brief conversation, the Mexican youth returned to his friends.

"He says the man we seek is Señor Miguel Santos," Tico said. "But luck is not with us, for Señor Santos is one of the villagers who disappeared. Only his wife remains at home."

"Where is it?" Frank asked.

"On the south side of the plaza, the one with the strange symbol painted on its door."

The boys quickly located the house. They examined the painted symbol for a moment, then Frank rapped on the door. It creaked open, revealing a thin, handsome woman. Her face was taut and pale.

"Señora Santos?" Frank asked.

"*Si*," she responded with a bewildered expression.

The boys introduced themselves, and after stating their business, asked the woman if she would help them.

Señora Santos seemed eager to discuss her husband's disappearance. She announced, much to the delight of the Hardys, that she spoke a little English.

"My husband and I once live in Mexicali," she said, forcing a smile. "We have much opportunity to learn your language there."

Señora Santos invited the boys inside and asked them to be seated in the tall wicker chairs that were scattered about the room.

"What can you tell us about your husband's disappearance?" Frank questioned.

"I know very little," Señora Santos informed her visitors regretfully. "One night he returns from a hunting-trip and tells me he see something strange in the mountains."

"What sort of thing?" Joe asked.

"He says that he see a group of men walking through the mountains," she explained. "Many were dressed like the Aztec warriors of old days. They were all chanting mysterious music."

"Did your husband talk to any of them?" Frank inquired.

"No," the woman replied. "But then some of the men see my husband. They chase him, but my Miguel escapes."

"When did you last see your husband?" Joe queried.

"The night he return from the mountains," she answered. "After eating his supper, he went to the *cantina* to tell his *amigos* about the men he see." Her eyes began to fill with tears. "My Miguel never come back. In the morning I find mysterious symbol painted on the door."

"What about the other villagers who vanished?" Frank asked.

"They are my husband's *amigos*," the woman said. "Each of them go to search for Miguel and never return. The doors of their houses are also marked with the symbol."

"And now the people of the village are too scared to do anything about it," Frank commented.

"That is right," Señora Santos agreed. "I should have

notified the authorities myself, but I do not wish to endanger the others in the village. Then when you boys ask me to help, I decide not to remain silent any longer. I know you try to help. I trust you."

The boys thanked the señora and returned to their camp, where Chet had already finished packing the equipment. "It's about time you masterminds got back," he blurted. "Did you pick up any information?"

The Hardys told about Señora Santos. "As I see it," Frank said, "the mystery is somehow linked to those men Señor Santos spotted in the mountains. It's a slim lead, but I'm all for going there and having a look."

"I'm game," Joe announced.

Frank turned to Chet and Tico. "Of course it's not fair of us to ask you fellows to come along on such a dangerous mission. If you want to . . ."

"What!" Chet exclaimed. "Me stay here without you? And who's going to keep you out of trouble? Count me in!"

"Me too!" Tico chimed in.

"Good," Frank said with a grin. "But we'll need more supplies."

"Maybe we can buy them at the general store in the village," Joe suggested. "Let's hope they'll let us in."

"If we are going into the mountains," Tico said, "I would recommend we use burros."

"Hold on!" Joe commanded. "We might not have enough money with us to swing it."

"Perhaps we can pay in traveller's cheques," Frank remarked jokingly.

The Hardys quickly examined their funds. Chet and Tico offered to chip in what cash they had.

"That should be more than enough to buy what we need," the Mexican youth observed. "Burros are not expensive here."

The boys returned to the village and headed directly for the store. Much to their surprise, the proprietor seemed too eager to assist them. He not only sold them the supplies they needed, but he also arranged for the purchase of burros at a reasonable price.

"The proprietor certainly went out of his way to help us," Joe commented.

"Naturally," Frank replied. "He and the villagers are glad to get rid of us."

Shortly the boys were off on their journey towards the distant mountains. As they jogged along, the terrain became more difficult to travel.

"This must be the slowest form of transportation in the world," Chet said as he tried to get his burro to move faster.

"These animals are slow," Tico explained. "But they are reliable and sure-footed."

The air became cooler as the riders moved higher into the mountains. Near sunset, Frank suggested that they stop and make camp.

"There's a flat piece of ground over there," Joe observed.

It was dark by the time they had pitched their tent and gathered firewood to cook supper.

Chet struck a match and was about to light the tinder when Frank suddenly hissed, "Put that out!"

"What's the matter?" Chet asked, flicking out the glow.

"I see a campfire!"

"Where?" Joe asked.

"On the other side of that gully. About half a mile away!"

"Maybe it's a party of hunters," Tico suggested. "There are mule deer, antelope and mountain lions in this area."

"Could be," Frank answered cautiously. "Then again, it might not be. We'll have to check it out. Chet, you and Tico stay here and guard the camp. And don't light a fire. We'll be back as soon as we can."

"Be careful," Tico warned. "The ground is dangerous."

Frank and Joe started off, moving slowly across the craggy terrain. In places the ground was gouged with narrow crevices and holes. They worked their way up a slope, then across a level stretch covered with tangled brush. Finally they dropped to hands and knees and crawled the rest of the way.

"There's the campfire in that clearing just ahead," Joe whispered. "Keep your head down!"

As the excited boys crept closer, a weird sound of chanting voices drifted to their ears.

·11·

Mountain Pursuit

THE sound sent a chill through the Hardys! Was this the strange music Santos had told his wife about?

More cautious than ever, Frank and Joe crawled forward on elbows and stomachs. In a few minutes they had the campfire in sight. Seated around it were eight men. Two, who wore sombreros and sarapes, were not Indians, but the others appeared to be Indians. Their colourful garb looked like that worn by the ancient Aztec tribe.

Beyond the fire and barely perceptible in its glow stood an Indian, with a rifle nestled in the crook of his arm. He seemed to be guarding the prone figure of a man, wrapped in a blanket and lying on the ground beside him.

Suddenly the two men wearing the sombreros got to their feet and began walking towards the spot where the boys were hiding. Quickly Frank and Joe moved behind a clump of brush and waited, their hearts pounding.

The two men came to a stop within a few feet of them. "*No me queda bien,*" one said.

Fearing they might have been discovered, the Hardys poised themselves for action.

"Sh—speak English, *amigo,*" the man's companion

ordered. "If the others hear us, they will not know what we talk about."

"I do not care," the first man replied defiantly. "Pavura does not frighten me. He has broken his promise. We were to be paid for our work. Yet I have not seen a single peso."

The boys gave inward sighs of relief! The men were unaware of their presence!

"Let us speak to Pavura when we return with the American," said the second man. "We will demand payment!"

The two men returned to the campfire, and the Hardys crept back to their own camp and reported what they had learned.

"You say they have an American with them?" Chet said.

"Yes," Frank replied. "He must be the one we spotted lying on the ground."

"I wonder who he is," Chet said.

"Will you try to rescue him?" Tico inquired.

"Not right away," Frank replied. "First we're going to follow those men and see where they're going."

"In rough country like this?" Chet countered. "Impossible."

"I can be of help to you," Tico said. "My grandfather was Indian. As a young child he taught me much about tracking. I am sure I can follow their trail."

Frank outlined a plan. He, Joe and Tico would go to keep an eye on the men. When their quarry made ready to leave, Joe would return to their own camp and tell Chet.

"Tico and I will mark a clear trail for you two as we go along," Frank told his brother. "You can then follow us at a safe distance with our burros and equipment."

"Sounds like a workable plan to me," Joe commented. "By the way, I noticed those fellows didn't have any horses or burros. They must be travelling on foot."

"That'll make it a lot easier for us," Frank concluded.

Since the situation prevented them from lighting a fire, the boys had a cold supper of canned meat and vegetables. Then Frank started back across the gully with his brother and Tico. When they spotted the encampment, they saw that the men had gone to sleep. One Indian remained awake to stand guard.

"We have a long night ahead of us," Frank said in a hushed voice. "Let's rotate a watch. I'll take the first shift. You two get some sleep."

At dawn the camp suddenly became alive with men scurrying about. Tico, who was the last to keep watch, shook his companions awake.

"I believe the men prepare to leave," he whispered excitedly.

Frank and Joe spied on the activity. One of the two men, wearing a sombrero and sarape, walked over to the prone figure wrapped in a blanket.

"I think you have enough siesta, señor," the man snapped sarcastically. "We go now." He pulled off the blanket to reveal a thin, grey-haired bespectacled man, tied hand and foot.

Elmer Tremmer! The Hardys gasped at the sight of

the pathetic figure, whom they recognized from a photograph in their father's dossier.

"Why did you tie me up?" Tremmer complained timidly. "I wasn't trying to run away!"

The man with the sombrero bent down and untied him. "I take no chances. Pavura would not like it if we return without you." He then pulled his prisoner to his feet.

According to plan, Joe hurried off to rejoin Chet. Frank and Tico watched as their quarry broke camp and headed in a direction that would take them deeper into the mountains.

"We'll give them a head start," Frank remarked.

Tico proved to be an excellent tracker. He quickly picked up the trail and followed it with ease. Frank marked their course by forming directional arrows on the ground with stones and twigs.

It was just about midday when Tico suddenly came to a halt. "Look!" he said in a low voice. "There are the men!"

Just ahead Frank saw their quarry. The men were seated on the ground. One Indian was distributing dried maize among them.

"They've stopped to eat," Frank said. "We'd better do the same, Tico."

The boys pulled several cans of rations from their pockets and ate quickly, then waited until the men set off again. It was almost dark before Frank and Tico had their quarry in sight once more.

The men were assembled in a clearing surrounded by steep, rugged hills. At the base of one hill was a large boulder which several Indians shoved aside.

Behind it was the entrance to a cave. The men entered, pushing Tremmer ahead of them. Several Indians remained outside to replace the boulder and stand guard.

"This is their hideout!" Frank said excitedly. "Let's backtrack and meet Joe and Chet before they reach this spot. The burros are likely to make a noise and give us away."

Returning along the trail, the two boys travelled nearly a mile before they met the others.

"Leaping lizards!" Joe exclaimed as his brother told where the trail had led. "You say they went into a cave?"

"That's right," Frank answered. "Let's reconnoitre the area in the morning. Maybe we can find out what they're up to."

The boys made camp close by and ate supper. All slept soundly. Shortly before dawn, Frank awakened and aroused the others.

"We'll go back to the place where Tico and I spotted the cave," he said. "It'll be better if we go before daylight. Also, one of us will have to stay here and guard the camp and burros."

"I guess I'm elected again," Chet grumbled.

Tico observed his expression of disappointment. "I shall stay here," he announced with a smile.

The Hardys started out with Chet along the marked trail. When they arrived at their destination, they selected a hiding-place from where they could view the cave. Within the hour the sun began to appear above the crest of the mountains.

"There are the Indian guards," Frank whispered as light spilled into the clearing.

"They're all asleep," Joe observed.

"Those guys don't seem to be taking their jobs seriously," Chet added.

"Obviously they don't expect outsiders to be roaming through these mountains," Frank said.

Finally the guards began to awaken. They scrambled to their feet and rolled aside the boulder covering the cave entrance. Soon, about forty Indians emerged and hurried off as if on an urgent mission.

"Look at all those men," Joe hissed. "Where could they be headed?"

The boys watched as the guards went into the cave and, seconds later, reappeared with Tremmer. They marched off after the others, leaving only one man behind. The Indian found a shady spot at the edge of the clearing and promptly went to sleep again.

"Now's our chance to take a look inside," Joe whispered.

The boys crept from their hiding-place and across the clearing. They froze in their tracks when the sleeping Indian grunted, but he did not wake up.

When they reached the cave entrance, Frank whispered, "Be careful. There might still be someone in there."

The searchers crept cautiously through the entrance. Inside they found a spacious cavern. Through the gloom, faintly illuminated by several nearly burned-out torches, the boys saw that the cave was empty.

Joe suddenly grasped his brother's arm. "Look! In the centre of the floor! It's the symbol!"

They all stared in awe at a large stone altar. On it was carved a cluster of branches or faggots. And mounted on top was a stone inscribed with the letter P.

Quietly Joe climbed up the side of the altar. At the top, he saw that a deep, circular channel had been cut into the stone. Charred bits of wood indicated that the channel was used to hold a fire.

"Holy crow!" he said to himself. "I wonder if this is some kind of cult."

Frank, meanwhile, in searching for clues, came upon a large section of damaged stone at the base of the altar. The broken fragment had been set back loosely into place. He pulled it away slightly and peered in through the opening.

The lower portion of the altar proved to be hollow.

"Hey, fellows!" Frank whispered. "Take a look at this."

"*Caramba!*" Chet exclaimed. "And see this, Frank." He moved towards the far corner of the cave. In the shadows was a stack of empty wooden crates marked MACHINERY.

"These look like the same type of boxes we saw being loaded aboard the submarine in the cove," Frank said.

Nearby were a number of small wooden barrels with the word *muestra* painted on their sides.

"*Muestra!*" Joe remarked. "That means 'sample' in Spanish, doesn't it?"

Frank nodded, then sniffed at one of the barrels. "Smells like crude oil to me," he muttered.

"What a discovery!" said Chet. "Come on. Let's look round some more."

At the rear of the cave, Frank found a cavity in the wall. Its opening was covered by a door of metal bars.

"Looks like a prison cell," said Joe.

At that moment Frank spotted a small fragment of paper on the floor. He picked it up. There was a single line of print:

The practicability of the draco . . .

"This must have been part of a page from a magazine," he said, handing the fragment to his brother.

Joe examined it. "You might be right," he agreed. "Too bad we don't have the rest of it."

"I'd like to see the complete spelling of the last word which begins with draco," Frank commented. "Something about it rings a small bell! I'm—"

"Listen!" Chet interrupted. "I hear something!"

The boys remained perfectly quiet for a moment.

"I hear it too!" Joe said finally. "Men talking!"

The three darted towards the entrance but halted abruptly when they saw the shadows of three men on the ground outside.

"Oh, oh!" Frank whispered. "It must be the guards!"

"And they're armed," Joe added. "It would be too risky to try and make a break for it now."

"But we can't stay here!" Chet whispered nervously. "That crowd of Indians might come back any time now."

Chet's fears were warranted. Soon many men could be heard approaching the cave entrance. The boys frantically searched for a place to hide.

"Quick!" Frank commanded, remembering the altar. "Follow me!" He pulled aside the broken fragment of stone at its base. "Inside! Hurry!"

The boys squeezed through the opening and into the

hollow portion of the altar. A split second later the Indians poured into the cave.

"*Fuego!*" one of them shouted. "*Fuego por Pavura!*"

The boys were horror-stricken. The Indians were about to build a fire on top of the altar!

·12·

The Search

"WE'LL be roasted alive!" Chet quavered.

"Quiet," Joe warned, nudging Chet with his elbow.

Frank fully realized their desperate situation. If they left their hiding-place—capture! Yet to remain—destruction!

The fire was started, and the boys waited tensely for the temperature to rise. But much to their surprise, the heat was not intolerable.

"Of course!" Frank said to himself. "The altar is made out of volcanic rock. It is radiating the heat of the fire too rapidly to get very hot itself!"

From outside came the same kind of weird chanting they had heard the previous night.

"They must be performing some kind of ceremony," Joe whispered into his brother's ear.

Suddenly the chanting stopped.

"Pavura! Pavura!" the Indians shouted in unison.

The deep voice of a man, obviously that of their leader, addressed them in Spanish.

"What's he saying?" Chet hissed.

"I can only pick up a few words," Frank whispered. "He thanks them for their work, and says they'll be rewarded soon."

After the ceremony the Indians left. Their footfalls faded away. Frank was about to push the broken stone aside when he suddenly stopped at the muffled voices of two men speaking in English.

"Why am I being treated like a prisoner?" one man asked.

"You tried to run away, Señor Tremmer," the other replied. "Perhaps you go to the authorities. I do not like that."

"You're wrong, Vincenzo! I didn't try to run away! Didn't I come to Mexico with you of my own free will? I just went out for a walk and got lost."

"Odd, then," Vincenzo replied, "that my men find you more than a day's journey from here. I do not believe you. However, I will give you one more chance. But if you run away again, I shall send my men after you with orders *not* to bring you back."

"Don't threaten me, Vincenzo!"

"Ah, but I will. And do not speak my name in the presence of my men. To them I am known only as Pavura!"

Vincenzo and Pavura! One and the same! The boys quivered with excitement. And Vincenzo was the leader of the Indians, who worshipped him.

More footsteps. Then silence.

"They've gone!" Joe whispered.

The boys cautiously crawled from their hiding-place and edged towards the cave exit. Seeing no sign of the guards, they dashed across the clearing and headed back to their own camp. After eating and taking a short rest, the young detectives mulled over the situation and discussed a new plan.

"Tico, you take one of the burros and go back to Montaraz," Frank instructed him. "Ask Señora Santos to help you get in touch with the authorities. Tell them what we've found out."

"*Si*, I will do as you say," the Mexican youth promised. "But what do you plan to do?"

"Chet will guard the camp, while Joe and I reconnoitre the area," Frank explained. "We'd like to find out what those Indians are up to."

After Tico departed for the village, the Hardys began a systematic search of the surrounding territory. They carefully threaded their way across the difficult, lunar-like terrain.

"When the Indians leave the cave," Joe said, pointing off to his right, "they go in that direction."

"Right," Frank agreed. "But let's stay close to this ridge. The rocks will give us good cover."

Nearly an hour had passed before the boys heard sounds of activity somewhere ahead of them.

"What's that?" Joe asked curiously.

"Sounds like men digging," Frank replied.

The Hardys continued on slowly. Soon they came upon a startling scene. In a small clearing ahead, Indians were working busily. Some were digging with picks and shovels. Others carried heavy wooden crates.

"Looks like some kind of mining operation," Frank said in a hushed voice.

The boys crept ahead for a closer look. They saw several Mexicans, not dressed as Indians, assembling various pieces of machinery. Nearby was a narrow-gauge railroad that stretched out of sight down an incline to the east. Resting on the track was an unusual-looking vehicle. It was an elongated wooden platform with sides that angled outwards and was set on eight small railroad-type wheels.

"What's that?" Joe blurted.

"I've never seen anything like it used in mining," Frank whispered. "It must be ninety feet long."

"And about six feet wide," Joe added.

"Let's work our way round to the other side of the clearing. Be careful. We don't want to run into any of these guys."

The boys edged their way along, studying the scene with increasing interest. Then Frank began to sniff the air. "I smell crude oil."

"I do too," Joe said.

Just then the Hardys heard a man shout from somewhere behind them. "*Pare!*—Halt!"

The boys whirled to see an Indian with a rifle standing at the top of a knoll.

"We've been spotted!" Joe gasped.

A shot rang out, and the Hardys ran. More shots. A bullet ricocheted off a rock close by.

"Head for the ridge!" Frank cried.

By now the Indians in the clearing had dropped their tools and were racing off in pursuit of the boys.

Joe stumbled and fell. Frank stopped and yanked him to his feet. "Are you all right?"

"Yes—I'm okay! Let's keep going!"

In the next instant the Hardys were startled to see several more Indians blocking their path to the ridge.

"This way!" Joe shouted as he started down a slope to the right.

The boys zigzagged through the craggy terrain.

After a gruelling race, they gradually outdistanced their pursuers.

"We're losing them!" Frank shouted.

Despite their exhaustion, the boys forced themselves to maintain their rapid pace. But they had travelled only a little farther when they suddenly came to a halt.

"It can't be!" Joe yelled, pointing directly ahead.

There was the clearing where they had spotted the Indians.

The youths had run in a complete circle. Soon shouts began to come from all sides.

"We're surrounded!" Joe cried out in dismay.

· 13 ·

A Charging Donkey

As the Hardys ran towards the clearing, Joe moaned, "We're trapped!"

"Hold on!" Frank shouted. "We might have one chance—that railroad car! Maybe we can drive it out of here!"

Amid shots from their pursuers, the Hardys darted to the odd vehicle, which was anchored by two heavy chains. They quickly unfastened the car and pushed it down the slope with all the strength that they could muster. Once it had picked up momentum, the boys leaped aboard.

Bam! Bam!

Frank and Joe ducked as bullets thudded into the sides of the wooden platform. The car gained speed. Indians appeared along the sides of the track, shouting and waving their arms, but they were helpless to do anything. Soon the pursuers were left far behind.

The boys raised their heads to look about. They were travelling downhill at breakneck speed.

"Now, how do we get off this thing?" Frank shouted. "We're moving too fast to jump!"

Joe pointed ahead and gasped. "Look!" Farther down the slope the track came to an abrupt end. Fifty feet from there lay a stack of rusting rails, directly astride the car's path.

"There *must* be a brake system somewhere on this!" Frank said.

The ground rushed by in a blur as the boys frantically searched for a way to stop the car. Joe stumbled to the rear and looked over the side. Spotting a long metal lever just within reach, he grabbed it and pulled upwards with all his strength. The rear wheels of the car locked, throwing up a shower of sparks.

"I found it!" he exclaimed.

Frank discovered a similar lever on the right side and yanked up on it hard. The centre wheels of the car locked, also producing a geyser of sparks.

Anxious moments followed as the car continued to coast down the slope, but slower and slower. Finally it came to a stop a few feet short of the track's end.

"Whew!" Joe sighed. "That was close."

Frank mopped his brow. "If we hadn't found those brake levers, we'd have ended up in little pieces."

The boys leaped out and trotted over to the stack of rails.

"Apparently they're still in the process of building this road," Joe observed. "I wonder where the track will lead when it's finished."

"That's something we'll try to figure out later," Frank said. "Right now, we'd better get out of here. Those Indians are probably on their way!"

They set off at a brisk pace, and after about a mile, stopped to rest.

"Our camp shouldn't be too far from here," Frank commented. He took a compass from his pocket to estimate the direction they should head. "We'd better get back before Chet starts worrying."

When they reached their camp the Hardys found Chet propped up against a rock, whittling a stick of wood. He appeared dejected.

"I'm bored," muttered Chet. "When are you going to let me in on some action? I'm tired of playing baby-sitter to a bunch of burros," he complained.

Joe laughed. "We want to keep all you donkeys together."

Moving like a charging linesman, Chet dropped his whittling and tackled Joe below the knees. The blond boy hit the ground with a thud, then rose grinning.

"I guess I asked for that," he admitted ruefully, and added, "Chet, did you ever think of playing pro football?"

The horseplay lifted Chet's spirits and he listened eagerly as the Hardys told him about the runaway rail-car. Then he opened some cans of food and they ate, seated on the ground.

"I hope Tico had luck contacting the authorities," Joe remarked.

"Let's keep our fingers crossed," said Frank. "Mean-while, we'll stay here and keep an eye on the Indians."

It was late afternoon when the Hardys crept back to the spot from where they could view the cave.

"Oh, oh! They have more guards," Joe observed.

"Just a precaution," Frank surmised. "Vincenzo isn't taking any chances after his men reported a couple of outsiders in the vicinity."

"One thing is sure," Joe added, "we're safe here. This is the last place they'd expect to find us."

As darkness came on, the Hardys saw Tremmer emerge from the cave. He strolled casually round the edge of the clearing and sat down on a boulder.

Frank leaned close to his brother. "I'm going to crawl down there and try to speak to him."

"But he might give you away."

"I have a feeling he won't," Frank said. "But if anything does happen to me, get back to our camp and wait for Tico to return."

"Okay. Be careful!"

Frank crept cautiously towards where Tremmer was seated. He manœuvred himself into a position directly behind the boulder, checked to see if the guards were at a safe distance, then called out in a low voice.

"Elmer Tremmer!"

"Who—who's that?" stammered the startled book-keeper.

"Sh—I'm a friend," Frank assured him.

"*Qué pasa?*—What is going on?" one of the guards shouted.

"Er—er—nothing! Nothing at all!" Tremmer answered, turning his head away from Frank.

The guard appeared satisfied and resumed his conversation with a companion.

"Who are you?" the book-keeper whispered excitedly.

"My name is Frank Hardy."

"Hardy? The Bayport detective?"

"I'm his son. My brother and I are here to help you."

"Help me? How?"

"To escape."

Tremmer shifted uneasily. "No! I don't want to escape!" he said in a frightened voice.

"If you're afraid to go back to the States," Frank whispered, "don't be. The authorities only want you to testify as a witness in the stock-fraud case."

"But Vincenzo told me I'll go to jail. I . . ."

"Who is this man Vincenzo?" the young detective queried.

"He's a very dangerous man," the book-keeper warned. "He leads these Indians under the name Pavura. They're very superstitious and think he's some kind of god. When I first met him, he used the alias Cardillo."

The young detective was started. Another alias! So Cardillo, Pavura and Vincenzo were really one! Frank pushed himself closer to the boulder.

"What is he using the Indians for, Mr Tremmer?"

"I—I can't tell you. And I'm not going to try to escape again. If Vincenzo caught me . . ." His words trailed off. He got up and walked towards the cave.

Greatly disappointed, Frank rejoined Joe.

"Any luck?" Joe whispered.

"I'm afraid not," Frank answered, then told him about the conversation with Tremmer.

"He might go straight to Vincenzo and warn him about us," Joe said worriedly.

"I don't think he will. My guess is that Vincenzo scared him into coming to Mexico. He probably told Tremmer he'd go to jail with the rest of them if they were caught."

"While all the time he just wanted to get Tremmer out of the way so he couldn't testify," Joe declared.

"Right!"

"Do you think he'll stick with the gang?"

"I've given Tremmer reason to doubt Vincenzo," Frank said. "If he realizes he's only wanted as a witness, he might come over to our side."

The Hardys decided to return to their camp. It was dark when they arrived.

"Funny," Frank murmured. "I'm sure this is where we had our camp-site."

The boys exchanged puzzled glances.

"Chet!" Frank called in a subdued voice. "Chet!" No response.

"Where are you?" Joe called louder.

"This has got to be the right spot," Frank said in alarm. He pulled a pencil flashlight from his pocket and played its beam on the ground. "Look!" He quickly bent over and picked up a small object. "This is the stick Chet was whittling!"

"But there's no sign of him or the burros and equipment!"

Joe spotted footprints in the soft dirt. Their pattern was scrambled, indicating that a struggle must have taken place.

Meanwhile, Frank made another discovery. Revealed in the bright, narrow beam of his light was a small heap of ashes. "Chet must have built a fire after we left," he called out to his brother.

Joe felt the ashes with the palm of his hand. "Cold!" he declared. "This fire has been out at least a couple of hours."

"That means it would still have been daylight."

"But the smoke! The Indians must have spotted it!"

There was a hollow feeling in the pits of their stomachs. The boys knew that there was only one explanation for Chet's disappearance. He was in the hands of Vincenzo!

· 14 ·

A Threatening Message

"WE must rescue Chet—and fast!" Joe exclaimed. "No telling what Vincenzo will do to him!"

"Simmer down. Let's keep our heads," Frank advised. "If we end up getting captured ourselves, we won't be able to help anybody."

"Okay," Joe said. "But we can't stay here without food, water and equipment. I'd say our best chance is to start back to Montaraz as soon as it's light. We might even meet Tico on the way."

The boys cut some brush to improvise beds, and fell asleep. At dawn they began the long journey to the village. At one point they crossed a wide, parched stretch of desert plain. Their thirst became unbearable.

"I don't even see a cactus plant around," Joe said weakly. "We've got to have water."

"Try not to think about it," Frank advised. "Just keep moving." They plodded on.

A few minutes later the boys spotted an abandoned vehicle partially buried in the sand.

"It must be a mirage," Joe said.

"Mirage nothing. It's a jeep," Frank observed, and hastened to it.

"This thing's as hot as a griddle," Joe remarked as he touched a portion of metal exposed to the sun.

"Looks as if the driver got bogged down in the sand and had to leave it," Frank said. "This thing must've been here for months."

On the rear floor of the vehicle, Joe found several wrenches wrapped in a large plastic sheet.

"If only we could squeeze water out of these," he commented, trying to force a smile. He flung the plastic aside.

"Hey! Wait a minute!" Frank commanded. "Don't throw that plastic sheet away. It might be the answer to our problem!"

Joe eyed his brother curiously. He retrieved the plastic sheet and handed it to him.

"Yes! This might just do the trick," Frank muttered as he examined it.

"Are you sure the heat hasn't got to you?" Joe asked.

"I'm fine," his brother assured him. "I just remembered an article I read some time ago in a science magazine. It described a water generator which uses a plastic sheet just like this."

Joe's eyes widened. "Say! Now that you mention it, I remember you showing me the article. You start by digging a hole three or four feet across and about half that deep. Then you spread the plastic sheet over it and set a stone in the centre. This causes the sheet to sink and form an inverted cone."

"Exactly," Frank replied. "It's based on the principle that even the driest soil contains some moisture. As the sun evaporates it, the water vapour condenses on the underside of the plastic sheet. The droplets then begin to trickle down to the point of the inverted cone and fall into a container."

The boys grabbed a couple of wrenches and began scraping a hole in the soft earth. Frank removed a headlight from the jeep and broke off its stem to serve as a container. He placed it at the bottom of the hole.

"Now help me spread the sheet over it, Joe."

When the job was finished, Joe picked up a stone and laid it in the centre of the sheet, which sank down towards the container in the shape of a cone.

"Now all we have to do is wait," Frank said.

"How long will it take?"

"According to experiments, about a quart is produced every twelve hours. But we should have enough water to quench our thirst long before that."

The Hardys sat beside the jeep. Removing their jackets, they spread them over their heads in order to ward off the hot rays of the sun. After several hours they checked on the progress of their water generator.

"It worked like a charm," Frank said, pointing to the clear water that had collected in the container.

Joe grinned. "There must be at least a pint there."

Frank took the first swig. "Finest water I ever tasted," he quipped, and handed the container to his brother.

"You're right. Great stuff!" Joe glanced at the position of the sun. "It'll be dark within a couple of hours," he continued. "Let's try to cover a little distance by then. We'll take the water generator with us."

The boys got underway. Soon they found themselves

moving into an area where they saw increasing signs of plant life.

"I see some acerlo bushes!" Joe exclaimed. "They have those small red and yellow apples Tico told us about."

The Hardys picked a supply of the fruit and ate heartily.

"It's a far cry from Mother's or Aunt Gertrude's home-cooking," Joe commented, "but at least it'll keep us from starving."

Exhausted, the boys fell asleep and did not wake until dawn. As they continued their journey, Frank and Joe saw that they were moving into cactus country.

"We won't have to depend on our generator for water after all," Joe observed. "There's enough in those cactus plants to fill a lake."

As the Hardys were plodding over the top of a sandy knoll, Joe suddenly stopped and pointed. Frank looked down at the bottom of a shallow gully to see two Mexicans wearing sombreros. Nearby was a canvas lean-to for shelter, and over a fire was suspended a black kettle in which something was cooking.

"Just campers," Joe muttered.

"Maybe," Frank whispered. "But we'd better not take any chances. They might be members of Vincenzo's gang."

Unaware of the Hardys, one of the men picked up a walkie-talkie and began speaking into it. Under cover of the brush, Frank and Joe crept closer to eavesdrop.

"Montaraz! Montaraz!" the Mexican exclaimed. "*No comprendo! Repita, por favor!*—I do not understand!

Please repeat!" There was a moment of silence. "*Bueno! Bueno!*" he continued. "*Pavura aguardar!*— Good! Good! Pavura awaits!"

"Did you hear that?" Joe hissed. 'He's talking to someone in Montaraz. And he mentioned Pavura!"

Frank did not reply. He signalled for Joe to withdraw a safer distance away, and they crept back across the knoll.

"What did you make of it?" Joe inquired. "We're still several miles from Montaraz. That walkie-talkie can't transmit so far."

"My guess is that Vincenzo has a string of men, spaced just within range of one another, extending from his headquarters to the village," Frank replied.

"You mean a chain of communication?" Joe asked.

"Right! Pretty clever, too. If Vincenzo used a single transmitter at his headquarters, it would have to be more powerful. That would increase the danger of his messages being picked up by the authorities. This way the signal range is very limited."

"Why don't we grab those two guys?" Joe snapped.

"No," Frank answered. "It would cause a break in the chain and warn Vincenzo that something is wrong."

"Well, at least we've learned one fact. He must have a spy in the village."

The boys resumed their journey, estimating that they would reach Montaraz by nightfall.

"We'd better change our course slightly," Frank advised, "so we don't stumble across any of Vincenzo's men."

"They might be members of Vincenzo's gang!"
Frank whispered.

Tired and dusty, the Hardys trudged into the outskirts of the village shortly after dark.

"There's only one person we can trust in Montaraz," Frank said. "That's Señora Santos. But we must be extra careful. Now that we know there's at least one spy in the village, we can't risk being seen."

The boys crouched low and headed for Señora Santos's home. At that hour the streets were deserted, but as the young detectives skirted the plaza, a man emerged from the *cantina*. The boys darted behind a tree until he walked by. When they reached the Santos house, Frank tapped lightly on the door.

"*Quién vive?*—Who is there?" came the muffled voice of a woman from behind the door.

"The Hardys," Frank said.

"*Ah, los muchachos!* One moment, I shall open the door," announced Señora Santos.

"Put out your light first," Frank replied. "We don't want to be silhouetted in the doorway."

The woman obeyed. Then she admitted the boys and relit the small oil lamp.

"Do you bring news of my husband?" she asked hopefully.

"I'm afraid not," Joe said sympathetically.

"Has our friend Tico been here?" Frank inquired.

"No, I not see him," Señora Santos answered.

The Hardys glanced at each other worriedly.

"I do not think I see you again," she muttered nervously.

"Why not?" Frank questioned.

"This morning I find a note under my door. It say

I no speak with you if you come to our village. I not obey!"

"Is that all the message said?" Joe queried.

"No," the woman replied. Her face turned pale. "It say that your two friends are in the hands of Pavura. If you try to contact police, you never see them again, and I will not see my husband!" She burst into tears.

"Good grief!" Frank exclaimed. "Vincenzo has Tico as well as Chet!"

· 15 ·

Tunnel Escape

"Now we're really in trouble!" Joe declared.

"It's a cinch we can't go to the authorities," Frank said nervously. "We'd be risking the lives of Chet, Tico and Señor Santos."

The woman continued to sob and the Hardys tried to comfort her. "Don't worry," Frank said. "We'll figure out some way to rescue them."

"I'm for going back to the cave," Joe said.

"So am I," Frank agreed. "It would be better if we had some help, but we'll have to do without it."

"What about supplies?" Joe said.

Señora Santos turned to the boys. "I give you food, and my husband has things to make camp. You may take what you need."

She led the way to another room and pointed to a large wooden chest. Inside it, the boys found a pup tent, canteens, a small hatchet, and other useful items. Joe selected some rock-climbing tools, pitons and a coil of rope, and tucked them into his belt.

"My uncle lives three miles north of the village," Señora Santos said. "He is elderly and cannot help you. But he has horses which you may borrow."

"Thank you, señora," Frank said with a bow.

The woman jotted a note in Spanish, which she handed to Joe, along with a golden locket. "Give my uncle this," she instructed. "He will know I have sent you."

The Hardys decided to start immediately. They stalked out of the village and headed north. An hour later they found the hacienda of Señora Santos's uncle without any difficulty. The old man took the note and locket, spoke rapidly to the boys in Spanish, and beckoned them to follow him to the corral. There he provided them with two chestnut-coloured horses. The Hardys mounted and rode off, smiling and waving their thanks.

"This is sure better than walking," Joe declared.

"You can say that again," Frank replied. "But we'd better not try travelling too far in the dark. We'll put a little more distance between us and Montaraz, then stop to rest."

After they had ridden an hour, the Hardys made camp and feasted from a supply of *tortillas* and dried fruit Señora Santos had given them.

The next day the journey continued in a direction designed to avoid the men in Vincenzo's chain of communication. The ride was dusty, hot, and fatiguing. The boys pushed on, however, at a rapid pace and reached their destination late that afternoon.

"We'd better not get any closer to the cave than this," Frank advised. "Vincenzo is certain to have extra guards watching for intruders."

"Here's a good place to make camp," Joe said as he examined a deep cleft in the rocks surrounded by heavy brush.

"Good," Frank answered. "And there's enough vegetation around for the horses."

Next day, before dawn, Frank and Joe started out on foot towards Vincenzo's hideout. Cautiously they crept to the spot from where they could view the cave entrance in secret.

"They've doubled the guard," Joe observed.

"That complicates matters," Frank whispered. "But first we'll have to find out where Chet and the others are being kept before we can plan a rescue."

Just as the sun began to rise above the crest of the mountains, the Indian workers emerged from the cave.

"Right on schedule," Joe remarked in a low voice.

"And some of the guards are going with them," Frank said.

The workers were immediately followed by six Mexicans who were obviously captives. Two guards prodded them along with their rifles.

"They must be the men who disappeared from the village!" Joe whispered excitedly.

"I'm sure of it," his brother agreed. "One of them must be Señor Santos."

Suddenly something attracted Frank's attention. "That's odd," he muttered. "I hadn't noticed it before."

"What?"

Frank pointed to a ledge farther up the slope above the cave. Two Indians had just appeared from behind a curtain made of twigs and brush.

"It looks like the entrance to another cave," Joe muttered in surprise.

"Maybe that's where Chet and Tico are being held

prisoners," Frank surmised. "If we could reach that ledge, we could crawl along it without being seen."

The boys decided to make an immediate attempt. They scanned the area and elected to work their way around the east side of the clearing, then up the craggy face of the slope.

"There are plenty of rocks to give us cover," Frank concluded.

The Hardys inched their way along. Progress was painfully slow when they reached the slope and began the gruelling climb to the ledge. The boys' pulses quickened as one of the guards in the clearing below looked up in their direction. But he turned away without spotting them.

Finally the Hardys reached their goal. They flattened themselves out on the ledge and pushed their way towards the place from which they had seen the Indians emerge. Frank carefully lifted up the lower corner of the curtain woven from twigs and brush.

"What do you see?" Joe whispered.

"It's a cave all right," Frank answered in a hushed voice.

"Careful! There might be more Indians inside."

"I don't see any. We're in luck!"

The boys cautiously crawled in through the entrance. Then they got to their feet and examined their surroundings in the dim light. They were in a spacious chamber which narrowed towards the rear to form a corridor about the size of a subway tunnel. It appeared to lead deeper into the centre of the mountain.

"This must be another of Vincenzo's storage rooms," Joe remarked, noticing several rows of wooden crates.

Frank gazed curiously at a number of strange-looking, elongated objects stretched along one wall of the cave.

"These seem to be rubber-coated nylon containers of some kind," he said, examining them more closely.

"And they're about as long as that crazy rail-car we took a ride on," Joe added.

Suddenly the curtain covering the entrance moved aside. Two Indians walked into the cave. Unable to find a hiding-place in time, the boys crouched low.

"*Cuando estará listo?*—When will it be ready?" one of the Indians asked his companion.

The other was about to answer when the two men came to an abrupt halt. They stared directly at the Hardys with startled expressions.

"After them before they warn the others!" Frank exclaimed.

The boys sprang up and hurled themselves towards the Indians. They crashed into the midriffs of the men and sent them tumbling to the ground. Frank lashed out with a right that knocked his opponent unconscious. The second Indian broke from Joe's grasp. He darted to the cave entrance and shouted a warning to his companions. Joe rushed after him and dealt the Indian a blow that sent him sprawling.

"How do we get out of here?" Joe cried as he and his brother heard the sound of shouting men drawing closer.

Frank peered at the long, dark corridor leading from the rear of the cave. "That way!" he ordered.

The boys stumbled through the inky blackness of the tunnel for a short distance. Then they pulled out their pencil flashlights and examined the path ahead.

"This tunnel might lead to a dead end!" Joe declared.

"We have no choice but to go on!" Frank replied.

Already many Indians could be heard entering the tunnel in pursuit. In desperation, the Hardys broke into a frantic run. Finally they had to stop for a moment to catch their breath. As the boys did so, they gradually became aware of a new sound.

"Do you hear that?" Joe asked. They listened more intently.

"Sounds like flowing water!" Frank replied.

Continuing on, they noticed that the sound became louder. At a point where the tunnel grew wider, the boys directed the beams of their flashlights a distance ahead.

Joe gasped. "Look! It's an underground river!"

They whirled to see the flickering glow of torches approaching from far down the tunnel.

"Let's chance it and try swimming downstream!" Joe suggested frantically.

"Okay!"

The Hardys quickly removed their shoes, tied the laces together, and draped them round their necks. They jumped feet first into the water. No sooner had the icy current swept them away, when several Indians arrived on the scene.

"They're not coming after us!" Joe sputtered.

The boys fought hard to keep their heads above the churning water as the river carried them through a dark tunnel. Minutes later they saw a bright circle of light ahead.

"Sunlight!" Frank shouted, but his joy suddenly froze to horror.

The underground river gushed through the opening and cascaded out of sight with a thunderous roar!

·16·

Face to Face

THE swift current tumbled the Hardys towards the river's drop. They were about to be swept through when Joe, in the lead, grabbed a segment of rock projecting from the wall of the tunnel about three feet above hs head.

"Hang on to me!" he shouted.

Frank clung to Joe's waist and gazed through the opening. The water cascaded to jagged rocks below.

"Don't let go!" he screamed, "or we're finished!"

"I'll hang on as long as I can!" Joe shouted.

The water pounded against the boys and threatened to carry them with it into the chasm.

"The rock-climbing tools!" Frank cried out.

Joe hooked his left arm around the projection of rock and pulled a piton from his belt. Using the small hatchet in his right hand and holding the pin in the other, he hammered the piton into the tunnel wall. Then he took the coil of rope and threaded one end through the eyelet of the piton to form a double line.

Grasping it firmly with both hands, Joe let go of the rock and slowly fed out line. With the current pulling the boys' bodies forward, they were swept outside the opening. They dangled precariously above the chasm as water gushed over them.

"There's a narrow ledge to our left!" Frank yelled. "It looks just big enough for us to stand on if we can get close enough to reach it."

He kicked out hard and the boys started to swing back and forth like a human pendulum. Frank, with only one hand round his brother's waist, reached out for the ledge with the other.

"Almost!" he called as they arched up towards it. Finally, after a hard swing, Frank managed to grab hold of the ledge. He and Joe pulled themselves up on to it. Then Joe released one half of the double line and pulled the rope free from the piton inside the tunnel.

"It's about two hundred feet to the bottom of this waterfall," Frank remarked. "And another two hundred to the top of the mountain," he said as he peered at the sheer rock wall stretching above them.

"And it's too far to the bottom for the amount of rope we have," Joe observed. "Our best chance is to try making it to the top."

Joe took one of his four remaining pitons and hammered it into the rock wall above the ledge. Using it as a foothold, he carefully lifted himself up. Then he drove another piton into the wall and repeated the procedure.

Frank began the dangerous climb immediately behind his brother. When Joe had used the last of his pitons, Frank reached down, loosened the lowermost one from the wall, and handed it to him. Each time the cycle was repeated, the boys edged a few feet closer to their goal.

Finally they reached the top and dragged themselves on to a level stretch of ground. "Whew!" Joe gasped. "I was beginning to think this hill was higher than Everest."

The Hardys rested for a moment to regain their strength. Several minutes had passed when suddenly they were startled to see the shadows of two men fall across the ground from behind.

"Oh, oh!" Frank muttered. "We have company!"

Turning round, the youths saw two Indians standing just a few feet away.

"You come!" one of them demanded. "*Pronto! Pronto!*" He made a menacing gesture with his rifle.

"Some of Vincenzo's men must've spotted us climbing the wall," Frank said to his brother.

"And planned this little reception for us," Joe added. "It looks as if they mean business."

The Indian repeated his order, then forced the boys to march in front of him. They slowly made their way down a steep, treacherous slope on the opposite side of the mountain. When they reached the bottom, the Indians took the captives back to their leader's hideout.

The Hardys were prodded into the cave and led directly to the chamber which served as a prisoners' cell.

"Chet and Tico are in there!" Joe exclaimed as one of the Indians unlocked the door of metal bars.

Frank and his brother were shoved inside and the door slammed behind them. Two Indians posted themselves outside as guards. Despite the boys' predicament, they were overjoyed by the reunion.

"Sorry I messed up your plans, fellows," Chet said

apologetically. "But I didn't think a small campfire would raise much smoke."

"It's too late to think about it now," Frank replied.

"What happened to you?" Joe asked Tico. "How were you captured?"

"I had almost made it to Montaraz," the Mexican youth explained, "when I came upon two men camped in the desert. They took me prisoner. One of them brought me back here after contacting Pavura on a small radio."

"You ran across a couple of men in Vincenzo's communication chain," Frank said. The Hardys then told the others about their own adventure.

"Juan, Marcheta's son, is being held prisoner here," Chet announced. "And also six men from the village of Montaraz."

"And one of them is Señor Santos," Tico added.

"That's what we figured," Joe said. "We saw them being taken from the cave."

"Did they say anything about what Vincenzo and his workers are up to?" Frank queried.

"They know only that they are made to work with the Indians on a small railroad," Tico answered.

"Why aren't you two forced to go along?" Joe asked curiously.

Tico grinned. "I overheard one of the guards say that Vincenzo thinks we are cleverer than the others," he said. "He does not feel it is worth the extra guards it would take to watch us."

"I'd say Vincenzo is a good judge of character," Chet muttered proudly.

Later, the Indian workers began to swarm into the

cave. Then Juan Marcheta and the six prisoners from Montaraz were returned to the cell. Tico introduced them to the Hardys.

Juan, a lean, dark-haired boy, told the young detectives how he had been kidnapped by Vincenzo in order to stop his father from co-operating with the authorities.

"Your father is in hiding," Frank told him. "I'm sorry I can't tell you where he is, but he's safe."

Santos, a tall, pleasant-looking man with a thick moustache, anxiously asked the Hardys if they had any news of his wife.

"We saw her just two days ago," Joe said. "She's well."

"Ah! That is good!" he replied with a sigh of relief.

"Why did Vincenzo take you prisoner?" Frank asked him.

Santos said he had accidentally stumbled upon the gang leader's hideout while on a hunting-trip. When he returned to Montaraz, he told some of his friends about his discovery.

"Upon leaving the *cantina* that night," the Mexican continued, "I was struck on the head and knocked out. I was brought here." He pointed to the other five men. "My *amigos* came to look for me and were also captured."

Joe remarked, "Obviously Vincenzo wanted to keep you from telling anyone about his hideout."

"And he put the strange symbol on the doors of your houses to terrorize the other villagers," Frank surmised. "It was meant to discourage them from getting curious."

An Indian appeared and handed each of the prisoners a plate of dried maize. When they had finished eating, the weary captives fell asleep.

They were awakened the next morning by the sound of the Indian workers as they left the cave. Several guards came and escorted Santos and the other five men from the cell.

The Hardys' thoughts turned to the possibility of escape. With Tico acting as their interpreter, they made an attempt to cajole their two guards into releasing them.

Joe creased his brow. "We're not going to get anywhere with those guys," he said.

At that instant two men entered the cave and approached the boys' cell. One of them was a tall, angular man with thinning black hair. His close-set eyes and sharp features gave his face an expression of evil. The Hardys recognized him as the Mexican they had encountered in Bayport.

"It's Cardillo!" Joe declared.

"You mean Vincenzo!" his brother retorted.

The gangleader's companion, a short, wiry Mexican, stepped forward. "You are in the presence of Pavura!" he exclaimed. "You do not speak unless he bids you to do so!"

"Don't give us that Pavura stuff!" Joe snapped. "We know his real name!"

Vincenzo glared at the boys. "You think you are clever," he snarled. "But what you have learned will not do you any good."

"I wouldn't count on that," Frank retorted.

"I have no time for idle talk," Vincenzo growled.

He stepped closer to the cell door. "You will tell me the whereabouts of Mr Hardy and Señor Marcheta!"

"They went fishing in Tampico," Chet interrupted with a laugh.

"You will advise your fat *amigo* to be quiet!" shouted Vincenzo's companion.

"I order you to answer my questions!" the leader barked impatiently. "Does your father know you are here in Baja?"

"You'll have to figure that out for yourself!" Frank replied.

"You force me to take stronger measures," Vincenzo announced. "Perhaps the fiery brand of Pavura will loosen your tongues!"

The gangleader signalled the two guards, who immediately prepared a small pit of hot coals. Into it, one of the Indians thrust what appeared to be a branding iron. Minutes later he withdrew it from the pit. On the end of the iron, glowing white hot, was the mysterious symbol.

"Now!" Vincenzo cried. "Which one of you would like to be the first to know the terror of Pavura?"

·17·

A Hot Mêlée

"You won't get away with this!" Joe shouted.

"Oh, no?" Vincenzo snarled. "And since you are so quick to speak, I think you should have the honour of being first."

Joe was led out of the cell and his hands were tied behind his back.

"He's not bluffing!" Chet cried in a quavering voice.

The gangleader signalled the Indian holding the branding iron, who then walked slowly towards Joe.

"Stop!" Frank demanded angrily.

Suddenly, in a lightning move, Joe darted forward. Head low, he smashed into the midriff of the Indian, who jack-knifed on to Joe's shoulder. Then, snapping to an upright position, he flung the man to the floor.

"Grab the others!" Frank shouted to his companions.

The guards had neglected to relock the cell door. Flinging it open, the boys sprang into action. Frank caught the second guard squarely on the chin and knocked him unconscious, then he quickly untied his brother's hands.

A wild mêlée followed. Vincenzo lashed out and sent Tico sprawling to the ground.

"*Socorro! Socorro!*—Help! Help!" screamed the gangleader as he started to flee from the cave.

Frank gave chase and downed Vincenzo with a flying tackle. They rolled across the ground, locked in a fierce struggle.

Chet, who had selected Vincenzo's companion as his opponent, had pulled the Mexican's sombrero down over his eyes. The stocky man ran round the cave frantically trying to pull up the hat.

"I hear men shouting outside! They're coming to help Vincenzo!" Tico exclaimed.

Several Indians appeared in the cave entrance. Joe grabbed one of the small barrels marked MUESTRA and hurled it at them. The barrel smashed against the rocky wall above their heads and drenched the men with crude oil.

"Nice going!" Chet yelled.

Joe picked up another barrel and threw it on to the pit of hot coals. It shattered, throwing up a huge orange ball of flame and thick smoke.

"*Aheee!*" screamed an Indian in terror as he saw the fire.

Frank pulled Vincenzo to his feet and flung him into the path of two Indians about to attack. The men crashed to the ground in a tangled mass of arms and legs.

Meanwhile, Joe threw another barrel into the pit. The fire and smoke became more intense.

"*Salga! Salga!*—Get out! Get out!" Vincenzo shouted to his men.

Choking from the smoke, the Indians followed their leader out of the cave. Chet's opponent finally managed to pull his sombrero free and raced out after the others.

The boys threw themselves down and placed their faces close to the ground where there was a shallow layer of clear air. When the fire and smoke subsided, they got to their feet.

"Come out! There is no escape!" they heard Vincenzo shout from outside the cave.

"Isn't there anything we can do?" Chet asked nervously.

"Vincenzo and his men have us cornered," Frank admitted. He glanced round. "And there's no way out of this place except by the entrance."

"Come out at once!" the gangleader screamed. "Or I shall send my men in after you!"

With no alternative but to obey, the boys walked out of the cave. As they emerged, the captives saw that Vincenzo was in a mad rage.

"You're too troublesome to be kept here! I shall have you all sent to a place from which you will never escape!" he growled. "You're going to take an under-sea voyage!"

The boys were marched off with several guards prodding them along with rifles. Soon they were walking down a steep slope close to the narrow-gauge railroad the Indian workers had built. Frank and Joe noticed that the track now extended well beyond the point where they had stopped the speeding rail-car.

"Hm! They've finished the project," Joe commented.

"Yes," Frank agreed. "We wondered where it went. I guess we're about to find out."

"You no talk!" shouted one of the guards.

Finally they came to a cove on the east coast of the

Baja Peninsula. The Hardys noticed that the track continued to the water's edge. Nearby a group of Indian workers was seated on the ground as if waiting for something.

The boys' captors ordered them to sit down. Two guards were posted to watch them.

It was almost sunset when the Hardys and their friends were startled to see a submarine come to the surface out at sea. It slowly made its way into the cove.

"I can see the symbol on the conning-tower," Joe said in a hushed voice.

"It must be the same sub we spotted in the cove in Sinaloa," Frank added.

At that instant there came a rumbling sound. The boys looked to see several of the odd-looking rail-cars come rolling down the track. Each of them carried a sausage-shaped object measuring about one hundred feet long.

"They must be the rubber-coated nylon containers we found in the other cave!" Joe whispered to his brother.

Frank suddenly sat bolt upright. "Say! Do you remember the scrap of paper we found in Vincenzo's hideout?"

"Yes, I have it right here." Joe pulled a fragment of paper from his pocket. They again looked at the printed words which read:

The practicability of draco . . .

"The word *draco* must be *dracone*!" Frank declared.

Joe's eyes widened. "You're right! That must be it! I recall your showing me an article about dracones several months ago. They're rubber-coated nylon containers designed to carry oil. A whole train of them can be towed behind a ship!"

"Except in this case, they're being towed by a submarine!"

"So that's what Vincenzo is up to. He must be smuggling oil out of the country," Joe surmised. "But where is he getting it from?"

Frank thought for a moment. "My guess is that he got his hands on an oil-well. He's keeping it a secret to prevent the Mexican government from taking over control."

Chet was wide-eyed. "Vincenzo wants it all for himself! So he's selling oil to whoever will pay his price!"

The boys watched as the Indian workers began attaching triangular-shaped metal plates to the front and rear sections of the containers. The devices looked similar to the diving planes of a submarine.

"Very clever," Frank whispered. "Those gadgets are used to keep the dracones underwater when the sub is submerged."

The Indians eased each of the containers into the water and linked them together by means of a special cable. The long train looked like a huge floating sea serpent.

The boys were now ordered to walk towards the submarine, which had tied up at the shore of the cove. Then they were forced to get aboard.

"Lock 'em in the aft cabin!" shouted a bearded crew member.

After climbing down through a hatch, the Hardys and their friends were led along a narrow passageway, then ordered into a small compartment. The door was slammed behind them and locked. A guard was posted outside.

"Where could they be taking us?" Chet asked worriedly.

"We'll soon learn if we don't figure out some way to escape!" Joe declared.

"Let's think fast!" Frank urged.

Suddenly the boys felt a vibration and heard the rumbling sound of the craft's diesel engines.

"It is too late to do anything now!" Tico cried.

A feeling of panic gripped the four boys as the sub got underway. Where were they going? And what was in store for them when they arrived?

·18·

Outwitting a Crew

THE boys searched frantically for an answer to their dilemma.

"We must escape before the sub gets too far out to sea!" Frank declared.

Just then they heard the muffled voices of two men talking outside the cabin door.

"The boss wants you to stay here on guard," a man said. "I don't know why he picked you. You're always falling asleep."

"What's the difference?" the guard snapped. "Those kids are locked in. And even if they got out, where can they go aboard a sub?"

"Keep awake just the same," the other man warned.

Then silence. The boys waited and listened. Less than an hour had passed when they detected the sound of snoring.

"He's asleep," Joe whispered. "Here's our chance."

"But the door's locked," Chet said in a hushed voice. "We can't break it down—every crewman on this tub would hear us."

Frank glanced round. "We won't have to," he answered. "Our captors forgot one thing. The door hinges are on our side. All we have to do is force the pins out!"

Frank took a handkerchief from his pocket and wrapped it round the base of the hinge pin to reduce noise. Then he removed one shoe and, using the heel as a hammer, began to tap away lightly. Joe went to work on the second hinge.

The job was slow and demanded all the patience the Hardys could muster. Finally the pins were loose enough to be pulled free of the hinges.

Cautiously the boys eased the door aside. Outside they saw a grubby-looking man in a sailor's cap and jacket propped up against a bulkhead. He was sound asleep.

The boys pounced on him at once, and before the surprised guard could utter a sound, he was gagged, then bound, and dragged into the cabin.

"Set the door back in place," Frank whispered to Chet and Tico, "in case any of the crewmen come along."

"What's our next move?" Chet asked.

Frank rubbed his chin thoughtfully. "Somehow we must force the crew to turn round and go back to Baja."

"Maybe we can disable the sub," Joe suggested.

"Leaping lizards!" Chet exclaimed. "Don't do anything to sink us!"

"If only we could put the electric motors out of commission," Frank remarked.

Tico looked at the Hardys with a quizzical expression. "How could we then return to Baja without power?"

"Submarines have two sources of propulsion," Joe explained. "Diesel engines are used when travelling on the surface, and battery-operated motors when under water."

"If we could sabotage the batteries somehow," Frank said, "I'm sure the crew would turn back. They wouldn't risk going on without being able to submerge."

Joe glanced down at their prisoner. "I have an idea!" he declared. "The guard is about my size. I'll put on his jacket and cap and try to work my way aft. None of the crew expects to see any of us outside the cabin. I might just get away with ruining the electric motors."

"It's worth a try!" Frank agreed. "But we've got to work fast. Somebody might check on the guard."

Quickly donning the man's jacket, Joe stepped out into the passageway. He pulled the cap low on his forehead and cautiously moved towards the rear of the submarine. There was not a single crewman in sight. As he edged his way along, the humming sound of the craft's diesel engines gradually grew louder. Then the young detective spotted a compartment door directly ahead. It was partially open.

"That must lead to the engine-room," he thought.

He crept closer to the door and peered through the crack. There he saw a single crewman checking gauges and making control adjustments.

Realizing he had to act instantly, Joe leaped in through the doorway. The startled crewman whirled and hurled a wrench at him. Joe ducked, then sprang towards his opponent. He caught the man with a sharp uppercut that sent him crashing to the floor and left him unconscious.

"Now to put the motor batteries out of commission!" Joe thought.

He glanced about until he spotted a drum of lubricating oil. Joe shoved it close to the long row of batteries that operated the sub's electric motors. After quickly removing the caps which covered the battery cells, he pushed the drum over on top of them. Oil gushed into the batteries, and soon a thick, acrid smoke began to billow up.

At the same instant Frank, Chet and Tico were confronted by a crewman who had been sent to check on the guard. But before he could warn his accomplicies, the fellow was seized. In the brief struggle which followed, Frank kayoed him.

"Let's get out of here!" Frank whispered to Chet and Tico. "Head aft!"

They raced down the narrow passageway. The three had not gone far when they saw Joe coming to meet them.

"Go the other way!" he warned. "The engine-room will be swarming with men in a minute!"

Already the smoke from the oil-soaked batteries was beginning to cause a commotion aboard the sub. The frantic shouts of crewmen could be heard echoing through the passageway.

"We must find someplace to hide!" Joe declared.

Frank pointed to a compartment door just ahead of them. "That's the forward torpedo room," he said. "Quick! Inside!"

The boys dashed into the small room and eased the

The man whirled round as Joe leaped through the doorway.

door shut behind them. Seconds later they heard crewmen scurrying through the passageway outside.

"The captain wants everybody to report to the engine-room!" a man shouted. "Make it snappy!"

Joe clutched his brother's arm. "Do you feel a change in the sub's motion?" he asked eagerly.

"Yes!" Frank replied excitedly. "They're turning round. We must be going back to Baja!"

"Leaping sailfish!" Chet blurted. "Your plan worked!"

Tico creased his brow. "That is good," he agreed. "But we are still prisoners. How do we escape from here?"

At that instant the boys again heard shouts from the crewmen.

"The kids broke out of the cabin!" one of them yelled. "They're still aboard somewhere. Start searching every inch of this sub. Begin aft and work forward."

The boys grew tense as the crewmen began their hunt through the various compartments. Gradually the men drew closer to the youths' hiding-place.

"After you guys check the cabins, take a look in the forward torpedo room," someone ordered.

"We're trapped!" Chet muttered nervously.

Joe glanced round. "Wait a minute! There might be a way out of here!"

Frank immediately sensed what his brother had in mind. "You don't mean the torpedo tubes?"

"Why not?" Joe insisted. "By now we can't be too far from shore. I'll fire you fellows out through the tubes. I understand there's nothing to it."

"But it means leaving you behind," Frank retorted. "Nothing doing!"

"Don't worry about me," Joe replied. "I'm sure I can get away."

"How?"

Their discussion was suddenly interrupted by sounds of the crewmen getting closer.

"No time to explain now," Joe said. "This is our only chance. Hurry! Get into the tubes!"

Reluctantly, Frank, Tico and Chet selected one of the four torpedo tubes and climbed inside. Joe slammed the hatches shut behind them, grabbed the release lever, and fired. There was a loud whoosh of compressed air.

"What was that?" came the voice of a crewman from the passageway outside.

Joe flattened himself against the bulkhead adjacent to the compartment door. A split second later it was flung open and three crewmen rushed past the youth and into the torpedo room. Joe dashed out into the passageway unseen. He adjusted the cap and jacket and made his way amidships.

"Take it easy!" he mumbled to himself. "Don't look conspicuous!"

Joe located the control room, then climbed a narrow ladder leading up to the conning-tower. Several crewmen saw him, but in the confusion they obviously thought he was one of their group.

"The kids have escaped!" came a voice from below.

All the deck hatches had been opened to help clear the air inside the sub. Joe climbed out, jumped from the conning-tower on to the deck, and dived into the water. The craft glided on in the darkness, with the dracones slithering past like giant sausages.

Joe swam quickly towards the shore, which was silhouetted darkly against the night sky. It was not long before he sloshed out of the water on to the pebbly beach.

"I hope the others are all right," he thought, peering along the shoreline.

Joe began walking in a direction away from the cove where he knew the sub was headed. His concern for his brother and friends increased. Then he heard a familiar bird-call in the distance.

Joe cupped his hands over his mouth and returned the call. Shortly three figures loomed out of the darkness.

"Is that you, Joe?" came Frank's voice.

"Yes," his brother responded. "Are you fellows okay?"

"Just fine!" Frank answered.

"Speak for yourself, mastermind!" snapped Chet. "So being shot out of a torpedo tube is easy, you said. Next time I'll try it from a cannon."

"Chet just swallowed a bit too much water," Frank remarked, laughing. "So we rode on one of the dracones for a few minutes until he got his breath. Then we swam ashore."

After Joe had told of his escape, Tico said, "There are some awful mad men out there."

"Right! Now we must plan our next move," Joe said.

"I'd like to sneak back to the cove and see what's going on aboard the submarine," Frank replied. "But this time let's not get caught. Some of Vincenzo's Indians may still be around."

The boys edged their way along the coast towards the cove. Gradually they began to detect the jumbled voices of many men talking from some distance away.

"It's the sub's crew," Joe whispered.

Frank peered through the darkness. "The cove must be just beyond that low ridge of rocks ahead. If we climb to the top, we may be able to see what's going on."

As the boys started up the side of the ridge, they suddenly heard a metallic, clicking sound behind them.

"*Pare!*—Stop!" a man ordered in a hushed but determined voice.

The Hardys and their companions froze in their tracks!

·19·

The Trapper Trapped

TICO turned round, then looked straight ahead as the man uttered a rapid volley of words in Spanish.

"Who is he?" Frank demanded.

"I saw only the outlines of two men behind us," Tico said. "One of them has a rifle. He orders us not to turn round and to walk where he directs."

The boys were forced to comply. But much to their surprise they were instructed to walk away from the cove.

"If those guys are a couple of Vincenzo's men," Joe remarked, "we're going the wrong way."

"*Silencio!*" the man ordered.

The boys were marched towards a dense thicket slightly inland from the coast. On the other side was a small clearing. In the darkness the boys could make out the faint shapes of four horses. Nearby were three men dressed in military uniforms. One of them stepped forward.

"*Quién están ustedes?*—Who are you?" he demanded.

Tico told him that his friends were Americans.

"Ah, *Americanos!*" he said. "What are your names, please?"

When the Hardys identified themselves and Chet,

the man's eyes widened in surprise. "You are the sons of Señor Fenton Hardy?" he asked.

The boys were startled by his question.

"Why—er—yes, we are," Frank stammered. "But how did you—?"

"I am Lieutenant José Arandas of the Mexican Army," the soldier announced, adding that he was leading one of several units sent to Baja on special assignment.

He explained that several reports had been received about a mysterious submarine in the area. The Army had been asked to co-operate with the Mexican Coast Guard in an investigation.

"We were just about to make camp for the night," Arandas continued, "when one of my men saw a submarine offshore. I sent out two scouts to watch it, and now they return with you *muchachos*."

"But how did you come to know our father's name?" Joe asked.

"Señor Hardy recently arrived in Mazatlan to find that you were missing," the lieutenant explained. "The only information he was able to obtain was that you were last seen sailing off in a boat. But no one knew where you were going." The soldier said that Mr Hardy had notified the police, who in turn contacted the Army. All units were alerted to be on the lookout.

"We're sorry we caused Dad a lot of worry," Frank sighed, "but we didn't expect to be away for more than a couple of days. We'd like to get word to him as soon as possible."

"*Sí, sí*," Arandas said. "A helicopter will be in this vicinity tomorrow. We have a radio to talk with the pilot. He will relay a message to your father."

"Thanks," Frank replied. "And now, Lieutenant, I believe we can help you." The Hardys told the officer about their recent adventures in Baja.

"*Caramba!*" Arandas exclaimed. "And you say this *hombre* Vincenzo is smuggling oil out of Mexico?"

"We're certain of it," Joe assured him.

The lieutenant barked an order to his men. He then turned to the boys. "I go to the cove to seize the submarine and its crew!"

"Wait a minute!" Frank urged. "That would only serve to warn Vincenzo. He'd be sure to escape."

"Anyway, the sub is out of commission for a while," Joe added. "You can grab it later."

"Then you must lead me to Vincenzo's hideout," Arandas stated.

"We will," Frank agreed. "But you'll need more men than you have now to capture him and his gang."

The officer thought for a moment. "I shall contact our helicopter in the morning," he said finally, "and have the pilot instruct all other scouting units in Baja to rendezvous with us. Perhaps Montaraz would be the place to meet. I have already sent two of my men there to question the villagers."

Frank stiffened. "What?" he shouted. "You sent two men to the village? This means trouble!"

"I do not understand," Arandas said.

"We believe Vincenzo has a spy in Montaraz," Joe explained. "News of soldiers arriving there will surely send Vincenzo running!"

"Our only hope is to find the spy!" Frank declared.

"How?" Joe queried.

Frank quickly outlined a plan. They would rig up a directional antenna on Arandas's walkie-talkie and use it to obtain a bearing on the spy's radio signals if he should communicate with Vincenzo's headquarters.

Early the following morning the loud, fluttering sound of a helicopter was heard approaching the coast. When it came within sight, Lieutenant Arandas picked up the walkie-talkie and contacted the pilot. He first requested that a message from the boys be relayed to Mr Hardy in Mazatlan. Then he asked that the other scouting units rendezvous with him approximately one mile west of Montaraz.

When he had finished transmitting, Arandas handed the walkie-talkie to the Hardys. They quickly improvised a directional antenna from a length of wire and attached it to the radio.

"That should do it," Frank commented as he observed the rig. "Now, we'd better start out for Montaraz."

The soldiers mounted their horses. Each of the boys doubled with a rider and galloped off. Within a couple of hours the group arrived at the spot where Arandas was to meet with the other units.

"We'll go the rest of the way on foot," Frank informed the lieutenant. "If we come up with anything, we'll let you know right away."

"*Buena suerte!*—Good luck!" Arandas said.

Together with Chet and Tico, the Hardys rapidly walked the remaining mile to Montaraz. They did not enter the village, but posted themselves on the outskirts.

"Since we don't know what frequency the spy is

transmitting on," Frank remarked, "we'll have to keep sweeping through the entire band. We're close enough to the village to pick up a strong signal."

The boys patiently and slowly worked the frequency knob of the walkie-talkie back and forth. An hour passed. Then suddenly a conversation between two men crackled from the speaker.

"Can you make out what they're saying, Tico?" Joe asked anxiously.

"Yes!" the Mexican boy answered. "One man says he has an urgent message for Vincenzo. He warns that there are soldiers in the village asking questions!"

Frank quickly turned the walkie-talkie until the axis of the circular directional antenna pointed towards the village. He then manœuvred the radio to the left and right until the signal faded completely. At that instant Joe recorded the direction of the bearing with his magnetic compass.

"Hurry!" Frank ordered. "Let's go to another spot and take a second bearing!"

The boys circled the village for some distance, then repeated the procedure. Now the voice of another man came from the speaker. "Stay there and keep an ear open. Find out what they're up to and report to me." Seconds later the transmissions ceased.

The Hardys drew a rough sketch of the village to scale. Then they plotted the two bearing lines.

"They intersect at the extreme south-east corner of the village," Joe said.

"And there are only two haciendas in that area," Frank stated. "That simplifies our search. The spy has to be at one or the other."

Frank instructed Tico to hurry back to Arandas. "Ask him to meet us here with some of his men as soon as possible."

It was already dark by the time Tico returned with the soldiers. The Hardys told the lieutenant about their discovery.

"We must search the haciendas at once!" Arandas declared.

The boys and the three soldiers made their way towards the south-east corner of the village. As they edged towards their goal, they saw two rundown houses. They were in darkness and there was not a sound.

"Nobody home," Joe whispered.

"Let's split up into two groups and search each of the homes," Frank said.

Chet, Tico and two of the soldiers crept towards one structure, while the Hardys and Arandas headed for the other. Frank carefully lifted the latch on the door and it eased open. He and the others stepped into an untidy room.

They pulled out their pencil flashlights and began a search. Arandas posted himself at the door.

After they had searched for several minutes, Joe sighed. "There's nothing here to give us a lead."

Frank walked over to a large earthen jar resting in a corner of the room. Reaching inside, he let out a cry of surprise.

"We've come to the right place!" he exclaimed "Look what I've found!" He pulled out a walkie talkie.

"Tell the others to call off their search," Frank told

Joe. Soon Chet and the others arrived to inspect Frank's discovery.

"I wonder where the spy is now," Tico said.

"Maybe he flew the coop," Chet suggested.

"Possibly," Frank replied. "But we'll wait for a while and hope he shows up."

The watchers sat quietly in the darkened room. Less than an hour had passed when they heard the door latch being lifted. Then a short, stocky Mexican entered the room.

"Grab him!" Joe yelled.

The startled man cried out as two of the soldiers seized him. The boys directed the beams of their flashlights into the frightened man's face.

Frank blurted out, "He's the guy who threatened us with a machete the first time we came to the village!"

Arandas was about to question him when the Mexican, slithering like a cornered snake, broke away from the soldiers. He leaped through an open window and headed for the centre of the village, with the boys after him. Arandas pulled out his pistol but held his fire as the fugitive and his pursuers became blurred in the darkness.

The fleeing man raced across the plaza towards the *cantina*. In front of the building were two saddled horses. The fugitive leaped on to one and galloped off. Frank, who was closest to him, quickly mounted the second and started after him.

It was a bright moonlit night, so Frank had no difficulty keeping the escapee in sight. Gradually he closed the gap between them. As the chase continued, the young detective was startled to see about a dozen horsemen appear on the crest of a hill. Before Frank had a chance to wheel his mount round, he and his quarry were surrounded by the riders.

"They look like some of Vincenzo's men!" Frank thought. The man he had been chasing was obviously known to the riders. He whispered something to a lanky horseman, who then approached Frank.

"You are one of zee Hardeez," he said. "Pavura weel want to see you! You come!"

He grabbed the reins of Frank's horse and started off. The other riders trailed behind.

"We are going to Vincenzo's headquarters," Frank mused. "That's the first place Joe will look for me. He can lead Arandas and his men right to it."

But Frank's hope was suddenly shattered when he noticed that they were going in a direction away from the hideout that he and his brother had discovered.

"Vincenzo has relocated his headquarters!" he thought, trying not to panic.

Several of the riders behind him were dragging clumps of brush along the ground to erase the hoofprints. Not even Tico's tracking abilities could help him now!

·20·

Helicopter Capture

FRANK ruled out making a break for it. The odds were too risky, since many of the men were armed. Others carried walkie-talkies.

"These men must have made up the communication chain to Vincenzo's old headquarters," Frank thought.

With only a short rest in between, they rode all night. By morning their journey had taken them into a flat, dusty desert area. The sun was already intensely hot. Many of the men drank from canteens, but not one of them offered Frank a drop of water. By now he felt faint from thirst and hunger.

Presently the leader of the horsemen held up his hand. "Stop!" he shouted. "*Oiga!*—Listen!"

They heard a faint fluttering sound. Gradually it became louder. The men turned and looked back apprehensively. A helicopter shot into view from over the crest of a hill.

"*Caramba!*" one of them screamed.

The craft circled the group several times, then made a low pass overhead. Many of the horses reared up and began to mill round, stirring up thick clouds of dust. The startled riders completely forgot about Frank and galloped off frantically in all directions.

"Nice going!" the young detective yelled.

Shortly a second helicopter appeared. It hovered over the scene for a moment, then gently settled to the ground. Frank rode towards it as two of the occupants scrambled out of the cabin. His eyes widened in surprise when he recognized them.

"Dad! Joe!"

"Are you okay?" his brother asked anxiously.

"I'm fine," Frank nodded wearily. "But Dad! How did you—?"

"I received the message you boys relayed to me in Mazatlan," Mr Hardy interrupted, "and Jack flew me to Baja right away. There the Mexican Army had a helicopter waiting to take me to Arandas's camp."

"Dad arrived just in time to take part in our search for you," Joe said. "When the other helicopter pilot spotted the horsemen he radioed us and we flew here to see what it was all about."

The pilot of their craft, a young Mexican officer, called out to Mr Hardy and the boys.

"I am in contact with the other helicopter," he announced. "The pilot says that some of the horsemen are heading towards what appears to be a large encampment in the hills east of here."

"Vincenzo's new hideout!" Frank exclaimed.

"He is flying back to report to Lieutenant Arandas," the pilot continued. "He says we should return also."

Frank left his horse and the Hardys climbed aboard the craft. In less than fifteen minutes they arrived at Arandas's camp, which was now crowded with soldiers.

Chet and Tico ran to meet the helicopter as it

landed. They were elated to see that Frank was all right. Then the boys and Arandas discussed plans for the capture of Vincenzo and his gang.

"I shall have the helicopters fly my men to the encampment," the lieutenant declared. "Several trips will be required, but we will save much time." He ordered the airlift operation to begin at once.

"How about letting us go with the first group?" Joe asked excitedly.

Arandas grinned. "I know you are very eager to capture this Vincenzo," he said. "But I am now responsible for your safety. First let me transport my men, then you shall follow."

While the boys waited their turn, Mr Hardy opened a large carton of fried chicken. "I had this prepared in Mazatlan," he told them. "It's the nearest thing to home-cooking I could think of."

"Let me at it!" Chet shouted jubilantly. The appetites of Frank and Joe, as well as Tico, equalled that of their hefty comrade. As they ate, Frank asked his father about Señor Marcheta.

"He's still in Mexico City," Mr Hardy replied. "And while I was with him, he told me what he knew about Vincenzo."

The detective stated that Señor Marcheta had met Vincenzo in Spain several years before. The gang-leader at that time was posing as a buyer for a Mexican textile firm.

"It wasn't until the stock-fraud case came up," Mr Hardy explained, "that Señor Marcheta discovered Vincenzo was actually a very clever confidence man. He has been involved in everything, from selling stolen goods on an international scale to peddling worthless stock in a diamond mine."

Then the boys related their own adventures. Mr Hardy was surprised to hear about the oil-smuggling operation.

"That's a new one even for Vincenzo," he remarked. "He'll have a lot to answer for."

Finally Arandas announced that the Hardys and their companions could fly to the encampment. When they arrived, they saw that the soldiers had moved in on the gang. Indians were being lined up and questioned.

"Where's Vincenzo?" Frank asked quickly.

"He fled before we could surround the encampment," one of the soldiers replied. "We have men searching the area for him now."

Another soldier whispered something to Arandas. The lieutenant turned to the Hardys. "One of your countrymen is among the captives," he said.

"It must be Elmer Tremmer!" Joe declared.

The boys and Mr Hardy were led to a tent. Inside they found Tremmer in a state of panic.

"You've got to help me!" he pleaded. "I don't want to go to jail!"

"Then why did you run away?" Mr Hardy asked.

Tremmer nervously mopped his brow. "I was frightened! Vincenzo said I would go to prison if I testified. Please, Mr Hardy. I'm not a member of Vincenzo's gang! After all, it was I who sent you that note to beware of the mark on the door!"

"How did you know what it meant?" the detective queried.

"To be truthful, I wasn't sure," Tremmer replied. He explained that before leaving Bayport, he had overheard one of Vincenzo's men say an enemy had been dealt with—that he had received the mark on the door!

"I feared for you and your sons," Tremmer went on. "And again I sent a warning note to you at your hotel in Mazatlan."

Interrogated about the oil deal, Tremmer said the gangleader had learned of an old Indian legend which described thick "black water" of the mountain. Vincenzo guessed correctly that it was crude oil. While searching for the deposit, he had stumbled upon an isolated band of Indians. Being part Indian himself, Vincenzo quickly gained their confidence.

"Eventually they showed him the source of the black water," Tremmer continued. "It was a rich pool of oil which oozed to the surface and did not have to be drilled."

When Frank asked who was buying the oil, he was told that several Latin-American groups were bidding for it.

"The price was high," the prisoner said, "but still Vincenzo was making a big profit."

"Quite an operation," Mr Hardy remarked. "It must have cost a lot of money to set up."

"Most of it came from the Costa Químico stock fraud," the book-keeper admitted.

Leaving Mr Hardy to continue his detailed questioning, the four boys left the tent and were greeted by the villagers who had been kidnapped from Montaraz. With them was young Juan Marcheta. Amid voluble expressions of their gratitude, a rifle shot sounded, and soldiers ran towards the place where the helicopters had parked.

Suddenly rotor blades of one helicopter began to whirl. Seconds later it was airborne.

"*Caramba!*" screamed Arandas. "Vincenzo is a clever scoundrel!"

"What happened?" Frank asked quickly.

"Vincenzo was hiding nearby," the lieutenant answered. "He has just forced one of our pilots to fly him away!"

"We can follow them in the other helicopter!" Joe suggested.

Arandas pointed at the fuel tank of the craft. "Vincenzo thought of everything. He shot a hole in the tank. The fuel has already spilled away."

"Where could Vincenzo be headed?" Joe said.

"That helicopter doesn't have enough range to take him very far," Frank replied. "I've a hunch he's going to the cove to rendezvous with the submarine."

"Let's plug up the tank and go after him," Joe urged.

Arandas creased his brow. "It would not help to make such a repair. We do not have any more fuel available here."

"Then we must do it the hard way," Frank declared. "We'll use horses."

"But it'll take us hours to reach the cove," Joe argued.

"Maybe the sub crew hasn't finished repairing the damaged batteries," Frank spoke up. "The delay might be long enough for us to catch up with Vincenzo."

The Hardys, Arandas and twelve of his soldiers galloped off. It was already dark when they arrived on the coast a short distance south of the cove.

"Hadn't we better go the rest of the way on foot?" Frank said in a hushed voice.

"Yes," Arandas replied.

They crept towards a low, rocky ridge, then scrambled up the slope to the top, with an excellent view of the cove.

"The sub is still there," Joe whispered.

"But it looks as if the crew is busy getting ready to leave," Frank observed as he watched men, carrying flashlights, scurry round the deck. Their voices could be heard plainly in the still, night air.

"We must leave at once!" came Vincenzo's voice.

"But we haven't finished replacing the batteries," shouted a crewman.

"You can complete the work at sea," the leader insisted. "If we wait here until morning, the whole army will be on us!"

"There's not a moment to lose," Frank urged. "We must stop them."

"I shall have my men spread out and converge on the submarine from all directions," Arandas declared.

Cautiously they stalked towards the shore of the cove. Then, at Arandas's signal, the soldiers charged ahead. The crewmen were caught completely off guard. Chaos followed.

"There's Vincenzo!" Frank yelled. "He's climbing out of the rear deck hatch! Don't let him get away!"

He and Joe rushed after the thief. Two crewmen who attempted to intercept the boys were bowled over by Joe, and all three splashed into the water.

Frank kept after Vincenzo, who leaped off the deck on to the shore. As the youth closed the gap between them, the man picked up a small boulder and hurled it at his pursuer.

Frank ducked, then lunged ahead and struck Vincenzo on the chin with a straight right. The man crumpled to the ground in a daze.

"This is the end of the line for you!" Frank cried, yanking Vincenzo to his feet.

The action stopped as quickly as it had started. Arandas and his soldiers were lining up the crewmen on the shore of the cove.

"We found Arturo, the pilot of the helicopter, locked in a cabin aboard the submarine," the lieutenant told the boys. "He said he landed with Vincenzo just north of the ridge. I suggest you fly with your captive back to my camp near Montaraz when it's light enough."

The boys rested the remainder of the night. At dawn they took the handcuffed Vincenzo to the helicopter. The pilot started up the engine, engaged the rotor blades, and made a quick take-off. When they arrived at their destination, Arturo was dispatched to pick up Mr Hardy and the others.

"Hello, Dad!" the young detectives chorused as their father, Chet and Tico were delivered back to the camp.

"I hear you boys did a great job," Mr Hardy said.

"We were lucky," Joe replied.

"Did you get any more information from Tremmer?" Frank inquired.

"Yes," Mr Hardy said. "And he's eager to return to Washington to testify. We'll have to wait our turn with Vincenzo, though. The Mexican government gets first crack at him."

"There's still one thing I can't figure out," Joe said. "How did Vincenzo get his hands on a couple of submarines?"

"Tremmer told me about that too," his father answered. "He bought two obsolete subs in the States for scrap metal. Then he smuggled them out of the country for reconditioning. It wasn't difficult for him to dig up a few ex-submariners who weren't particular how they earned their money."

"By the way," Chet said, "I wonder what happened to the other sub you spotted in Barmet Bay."

"My guess is that it's headed here by way of Cape Horn," Frank said. "The trip will take several weeks."

"We'll notify the Mexican government to be on the lookout for it," Mr Hardy announced.

Leaving their prisoners with the soldiers, the Hardys, Chet, Tico, and Juan Marcheta were taken by helicopter to the small airport, where Jack Wayne was waiting.

"I just heard a flash you'll be interested in," the pilot told them. "The Argentine Navy boarded an unidentified submarine they spotted off their coast. The only markings it had was a strange symbol painted on the conning-tower with the letter P on it. They seized the sub and its crew."

"That winds up the case," Joe said with a wide grin. But he was looking forward to another challenging mystery to solve. In the near future, the young detectives would tackle *The Yellow Feather Mystery.*

Soon the Hardy plane was winging back to Mazatlan with happy news for Señor Marcheta.

"I'm sure Father will want to celebrate with a feast," Juan said.

"We're all for it," Joe said, laughing. "But don't have any bulls around. We don't want Chet getting more ideas about becoming a matador."